A Smoky Mountain Mystery

Steve Demaree

Steve Demaree

A Smoky Mountain Mystery

This book is dedicated to my wife, who is also my traveling companion, and to all of those who vacation in the Smokies, including those who look forward to each trip to Gatlinburg and/or Pigeon Forge. May the book put you on the edge of your seat, and may it make you yearn for your next trip to the Smoky Mountain area.

Books by Steve Demaree

Dekker Cozy Mystery Series

52 Steps to Murder
Murder in the Winter
Murder in the Library
Murder at Breakfast?
Murder at the High School Reunion
Murder at the Art & Craft Fair
Murder in Gatlinburg
Murder at the Book Fair
Murder on a Blind Date
A Body on the Porch
Two Bodies in the Backyard
A Body Under the Christmas Tree
Murder on Halloween
A Valentine Murder
A Body on April Fool's Day
A Body in The Woods
A Puzzling Murder
A Body in Pigeon Forge

Lt. Santangelo Mystery Series

Picture Them Dead
Murder in a Gated Community

Other Mysteries

A Body in the Trunk
✓A Smoky Mountain Mystery
Murder in the Dark

A Smoky Mountain Mystery

Aylesford Place Series

Pink Flamingoed
Neighborhood Hi Jinx
Croquet, Anyone?
Scavenger Hunt

Other Fiction

Stories From the Heart

Non-Fiction

Lexington & Me
Reflecting Upon God's Word

Steve Demaree

1

"9-1-1. What is your emergency?"

"It's my husband."

"Do you mean your husband is in trouble, or your husband is causing trouble?"

"I guess he's in trouble. We're staying in a chalet outside of Gatlinburg and I went to the grocery and came back and he's not here."

"Maybe he went for a walk."

"My husband doesn't like the outdoors. I was even surprised when he suggested that we stay in a chalet in the mountains for a couple of weeks."

"Are you in the chalet now?"

"Yes."

"Is there any sign that there has been a struggle while you were gone?"

"No, everything looks pretty much the way it looked when I left."

"And you've searched everywhere? The bedroom? The bathroom? Out on the deck?"

"That's right. He's not in any of those places."

"Have you looked around outside to see if he might have stepped outdoors and fallen? Maybe he fell down a hill. I imagine there's a hill near where you are."

"Oh, yes. We have a big drop-off on the backside, away from the road."

"Maybe he fell there. Can you see over the railing without falling?"

"I don't know. I haven't checked."

"Well, I'll hold on while you check. Check around the outside, see if you see any trampled grass where he might have fallen."

"Okay, I'm taking the phone outside. I have a high-powered flashlight. I'm up on a walkway with a deck on the second level. I can see everything from here. I'm looking. I don't see anything. I think you need to send someone out."

"There's nothing we can do until he's been missing for twenty-four hours. Just call the regular number if he hasn't come back by then, or call 9-1-1 if you find him and he's injured."

"Okay. Thanks."

"Remember to call the regular police line if he hasn't returned or contacted you in twenty-four hours."

"I will."

2

Archer & Carlucci is located in a two-story red brick building in downtown Lexington, Kentucky. There are letters painted on the front window identifying the business. But if you asked people who live in Lexington and work downtown what type of business Archer & Carlucci is, most of them would have a confused look. See, Archer & Carlucci doesn't advertise. Most Lexingtonians have never heard of it. So, if you stopped someone on the street and asked them what type of business they think it is, maybe some would ask you if it is a law firm, while others might say, "Sounds like an upscale store, Archer & Carlucci, Clothiers for Men." And if you told the owners of the business that most people aren't familiar with their company, it wouldn't disturb them at all.

Archer & Carlucci doesn't depend upon walk-in business to make money. Most of their business is outside of Kentucky. And both Jack Archer and Bernie Carlucci love their privacy. Both are married, Jack to Pam, and Bernie to Roz, but neither has children. And they don't belong to any clubs; not the Rotary, the Optimists, the Kiwanis, or the country club. They have no connections and have only been in the area for a little over seven years. And yet both of them are millionaires, with Jack living in a large home with acreage to the southeast of Lexington, and Bernie with a similar property southwest of Lexington. Both men are known for working all the time, but it's not that either of them is a workaholic. It's that neither of them trusts the other and would be afraid of what the other would do if he took a few days off. Carla Rogers, their administrative assistant can't remember either of them taking a vacation, but she doesn't know the reason why. Both men are married to women who are quite different than they are, and both men are about to leave on a trip, but for different reasons. Each of the owners is doing his best to make sure that no one finds out he will be away until after he has gone. One isn't even telling his wife.

3

Six Weeks Earlier

For years, Pam Archer wanted a vacation. Each year, as the weather warmed up, she had to listen to her friends talk of their upcoming vacation plans. And each year she had to make excuses for why she and Jack didn't go somewhere. All of her friends knew that she and Jack could well afford a vacation to anywhere their dreams desired. Pam didn't have a lot of friends, but that didn't keep her from longing for some time away with her husband. The only time she and Jack had been on a vacation was when they went on their honeymoon. And while it was an extended honeymoon that lasted just short of three weeks, it was so long ago that it's the only memory Pam has of a vacation as a married woman, and it's a distant memory.

From that point on it was business as usual for Jack. Like her friends, Pam too knew her husband could well afford to go anywhere he pleased and stay for a month, but he had always been reluctant to do so. Anytime she broached the subject, which was usually in the spring after her friends related their vacation plans, Jack told her to go without him if she wanted to go somewhere. At times Pam wondered if Jack had a woman on the side. But after years of sitting at home Pam's patience had worn out, and one night she confronted him yet again.

11

"We need to take a vacation."

"How long are you going to harp about that? How many times have I told you I can't take a vacation? I have a business to run, and I can't trust Bernie to run things for a week."

"If you can't trust him, why did you go into business with him?"

"I trusted him then. Now, I wouldn't be surprised if he tries to murder me to get my share of the business. It's worth millions, you know."

"That I know. That means you can well afford a vacation. But murder? I don't particularly like the guy, but murder is a strong word. Do you have any proof that he's planning to harm you?"

"No, Bernie's too smart for that. It's just a feeling I have."

"Well, you can't live your entire life worrying about Bernie. If you can't trust him, dissolve the business."

"Pam, that's a lot easier said than done. You know I can't do that."

"But you can take a vacation. Let's go away somewhere. Go with me for a couple of weeks and see how things are when you get back. You can even choose where we go. If we go away, and you don't tell Bernie where you're going, you should be safe while you're gone."

"Yeah, but will the business be safe?"

"Isn't there anyone there you can trust to keep an eye on things. What about Carla? Can you trust her?"

"I'm not sure. She a personal assistant to both of us. So far I haven't seen anything that says she's Bernie's girl, but I'm not sure I can trust her. At least as far as Bernie's concerned."

"Come on. Let's get away somewhere. Maybe you'll feel differently about things when we get back. Maybe you're just stressed and the stress is making you see things that aren't there."

"Okay. I'll think about it. If so, I need to hire someone to keep an eye on Bernie while I'm gone, check him out and see if I have anything to worry about. And I can't go too far away. Maybe somewhere where I can get back to Lexington by car in just a few hours."

"That sounds more like the guy I married six years ago. Willing to take a few chances, but not willing to do anything too stupid. Think about it overnight and come up with someplace we can go and enjoy ourselves. Just get away from work and responsibilities and have fun."

"I'll think about it. And I'm not sure I can get completely away from work. If I do decide to go, I'll need to take my phone, just in case."

"Sure, as long as you only take it along in case of an emergency, and don't use it to work the entire vacation. That's not a vacation. That's working in a different office so to speak, and right now you need to get away and forget about who's at home and what he's up to."

"I just don't know, Pam."

"Just think about it overnight. Let me know tomorrow what you decide."

"Okay. I'll call you from work sometime before noon."

+++

Pam thought Jack was sincere. She felt he was going to consider going away with her. He wasn't someone who had to wait until he got out of her sight to tell her he wasn't going anywhere. Jack could stand up to anyone. Not only could Jack be blunt, he usually was. Pam didn't care where they went, as long as they went somewhere out of state. She couldn't see Jack going to Europe, but not because he was afraid of flying. If she knew Jack, and she was beginning to wonder if she did, he would want to go somewhere where he could get back to work quickly, in case he was needed. Get back quickly. She was surprised he even came home at night. And while he came home every night, more times than not he came home late. And most nights when he came home early, he would give her a peck on the cheek, gobble down his supper, and head to his home office with a warning for her not to bother him unless it was important.

+++

Pam's suggestion got Jack to thinking. It just might work. He had one person he could confide in. He left the house, took a drive, and made a phone call. After he ended the call he had changed his thinking. This vacation thing might work. But he was still worried about Bernie.

4

Pam reminded her husband of his promise when he left for work a little after 8:00 the next morning. He nodded and mumbled something on his way out the door. She hoped he would see things her way. A little after 10:30 she had her answer.

"Pam, I just called to let you know that I've decided to take you up on your vacation proposal."

"That's great! Where are we going, or have you decided yet?"

"The Smoky Mountains."

"No, I mean where are we really going. I know you don't like a rustic lifestyle, and you're not into commercialism. And from what I've heard, most everything down that way is one or the other."

"You mean you don't want to go there?"

"I don't know. I haven't been there. We haven't been anywhere, even though we can afford to go anywhere we want. I think I'd like it, and if you're serious, I'm willing."

"I'm serious, even though you're right about me not liking anything rustic or commercialized. I'm thinking about dropping a few hints here in a couple of weeks that I'm looking into taking a vacation to Bermuda or Hilton Head, or someplace that has a beach. One reason I picked the Smokies is that there's no way Bernie will think I would ever vacation there. I've already hired someone to check him out, and I've booked our vacation for two weeks in the

Smokies. There will be some catalogs coming to the house for you to look through and see what you want to do while we're down there, but in the meantime check out some things on the Internet. And, just so you'll know ahead of time, we're staying in a chalet. Now I know that the word chalet sounds like something in Switzerland, but this one is not pretentious, but it's not all that rustic, either. It has three floors, a hot tub, a pool table, hiking trails nearby, and a great view across the mountains. And it's a half-mile from the nearest cabin, so we'll have our privacy. I'll show you some pictures of it when I get home from work tonight. and I'll try to get home earlier tonight than I usually do."

"Oh, Jack, this is so exciting! I can't believe you're willing to go somewhere!"

"Somewhere, but not everywhere. And I can't promise you I'm willing to go somewhere any time you get an idea that you need a vacation. And on this vacation, there will be some days when you can go out and enjoy yourself, go shopping, buy yourself whatever you like, while I stay back in the chalet and get some work done."

"So, when are we leaving?"

"I've got it booked beginning four weeks from Friday. We can't check into the place until 3:00 in the afternoon, but we can leave around 9:00, or so that morning, grab a quick breakfast on the way out of town and eat lunch when we get there before we go check out the place where we'll be staying."

"Sounds fine, but don't think I'm going to stay inside all day and do a lot of cooking. I'm planning on eating out, and acting like I'm actually on vacation."

"You will be on vacation. I'm doing this for you, but I'll need some space, too. I can't picture myself running around Dollywood riding rides and going to shows."

"Oh, is that where Dollywood is? I just thought Dollywood was what replaced Opryland. That shows you how much traveling I've done."

"Don't rub it in."

"So no Dollywood. And I thought I was going to lose you to the coasters."

"I didn't even do that when I was a kid. I was more into seeing how I could design one."

"Okay, so four weeks from Friday. I can hardly wait. We are driving down, aren't we?"

"Yeah, it would be too easy for Bernie to track us if we fly. And I don't plan to let anyone know that I'm leaving, so make sure you don't tell any of your friends. After we get there I'll call the office and tell them I'm going to be gone for a few days and I'm not sure when I'll be back. So, don't ruin it for me by running off at the mouth."

"Mum's the word."

+++

Pam ended the call and started thinking of her vacation. Were she and Jack going somewhere? They must be. He said he'd already booked the place. Were they going to have a good time? She hoped so. She didn't have much social life, and she couldn't think of anyone she knew who'd been to Gatlinburg. And she didn't know much about the place. Oh, she knew it was somewhere in the eastern part of Tennessee, but she wasn't sure what all was there. She knew there were mountains and a lot of tourists. And soon she and Jack would be two of them. Well, she wasn't sure about that. Jack might end up sending her out each day while he stayed in the cabin and worked. Maybe at night, he would take her to some out of the way place for a quiet, romantic dinner. Well, at least the scenery would be different. And she would do her best to get him to join her part of the time. Who knows? Maybe he would end up enjoying himself and decide that they would stay a little longer, or go somewhere else before heading home. Maybe they could recapture the magic she thought they had when they were on their honeymoon.

5

Pam thought that at one time she and Jack had a good marriage, but that was early. Now she wondered if that was ever the case. Oh, Jack had never hit her. They never argued much, and most of their arguments were about Jack working so many hours. At times Pam wondered if Jack was working all those hours, or if Jack might have something going with his secretary Carla. But then any time Pam had stopped by the office to see Jack, Carla never acted as if she had something to hide. If Jack did have someone, it had to be someone local. Jack seldom took trips out of town, and if he did and Pam asked to go along he told her he would be busy, but she was welcome to go with him. That didn't sound like a man with a mistress at a distance. But she needed to rid her mind of negative thoughts and think about the vacation that would be upon her before she knew it.

She was excited about the trip to the Smokies for two reasons. One, she couldn't remember the last time they took a vacation. It might have been their honeymoon in Mexico. Yes, she was sure it was. And she enjoyed it. But Jack had seemed to change only a few weeks after they returned home. But she hoped that their upcoming trip might rekindle their marriage. A cottage overlooking a beach or a chalet in the mountains seemed like the best places to get the home fires burning again. She hoped that

Jack remembered they were going on vacation and he wouldn't try to work the whole time they were gone.

Pam looked over the material that Jack brought home to her, and she checked out the websites online. And she spent a lot of her time shopping, buying new clothes for the trip. The hardest thing for Pam was not to tell her friends that she was finally getting to go on a trip. Well, she didn't think Jack would mind her talking about it after they returned. Then she could have lunch with her friends and tell them about *her* trip for a change. Maybe it wouldn't sound as glamorous as a trip to some south seas island, but she would build it up as much as she could to make them at least a little envious.

+++

A week or so before they left on their trip Pam drove downtown to Jack's office to meet him for lunch. He didn't want to give up his precious time, but she convinced him that an hour and a half wouldn't matter and that she wanted to run a few things by him regarding the trip. That was when she noticed some guy walk over to her SUV as she was leaving the parking garage, on her way to meet Jack. She noticed the same man when she returned. This time he was not far from where Jack had parked. She wondered if she should go back and tell Jack about him, but she didn't. Besides, the man was well dressed and carried a briefcase. Maybe it was a coincidence that he was there the same time she was.

+++

Two days before Jack and Pam left on vacation, Jack left the office to grab a late lunch. Just as he did, a car came speeding around a corner, jumped the curb, and would have eliminated him and his vacation if he had been texting instead of watching where he was going. When he saw the car coming right toward him, he dove into a doorway. The car missed him by less than a foot. He knew he didn't recognize the car and its tinted windows kept him from seeing who drove it. He stood up a few seconds later no worse for wear other than a little dust on his clothes, and an abrasion on his hand from where he hit the masonry of the building getting out of the way. By the time Jack realized what had happened and had turned to get a license number, the driver had sped off, turned another corner, and disappeared. Jack looked around to see if he had any witnesses to confirm what had happened, but there was no one. He couldn't believe something like this had happened in broad daylight in downtown Lexington and no one else was on the street to see it. Well, his office was a few blocks from the hustle and bustle of the center of downtown. Most days there wasn't a lot of traffic on his street. That's one of the reasons he liked his location.

As he stood there assessing his situation, he felt confident that his suspicions were right. He was sure that whoever bore down on him intended to end his life right there. It wasn't some little old lady whose license should have been taken away or someone who was paying more attention to social media than he was to traffic. It was someone who wanted to play pinball with Jack's body.

He refrained from calling the police, but before he headed to the restaurant for lunch he called the man he had hired to see if his partner planned to become the sole owner of the company.

"Someone just tried to make me a part of history. Know anything about it?"

"I didn't have anyone watching your back if that's what you mean, but I wouldn't be trusting that partner of yours."

"So far you haven't told me anything I didn't already know. What am I paying you for? Get me a name."

"I'll do what I can."

Jack ended the call and shook his head. Maybe he needed to take matters into his own hands. When he returned from lunch, he passed by Bernie's office. The door was open. Bernie was behind his desk, but he didn't have a look on his face that said, "You mean the guy missed you. Why am I paying him?"

+++

Jack was careful when he left work for the day, a few minutes after Bernie left. He kept his head on a swivel as he headed for the garage where he had parked, and he checked out the side streets and the rearview mirror on the way home. No one made a second attempt on Jack's life. He figured whoever it was would let it rest for a few days until Jack dropped his guard. But Jack knew something the hired gun didn't know. He wouldn't be around in a few days. He would be in a chalet in the mountains.

Jack didn't say anything about the incident to Pam when he got home from work, but he did consider leaving town a day early. In the end, he did nothing to change his plans, or alert someone that he was about to leave on a trip. That Thursday Jack behaved at work the same as he behaved any other day. He did not attempt to finish something he was working on. He didn't tell Carla that he might not be in the next day. He merely went to work like always and left at the end of the day. As far as he was concerned, it was an uneventful day.

+++

Pam was excited when Jack got home on Thursday night. She couldn't keep from talking about the trip, as if she was afraid Jack might have forgotten they were leaving the next day.

"You didn't tell any of those friends of yours that we're going somewhere, did you?"

"It was hard not to, but no I didn't, Jack."

"But with this Susie Sunshine attitude of yours, you might have given it away when you talked to them today."

"I didn't talk to anyone today except Helen, and I didn't give anything away to her. Besides, a woman can get excited about things other than going on vacation. Especially a woman my age. Maybe she would think that I found out I'm pregnant, but couldn't tell anyone yet."

"You're not, are you?"

"Jack, are you forgetting what it takes to get pregnant?"

"Well, I've been working late. I'm tired when I get home."

"I know. For the last five or six years, at least."

"Just calm down or I won't go."

"You try backing out now and you won't have to worry about Bernie doing something to you. He won't get the first chance."

That reminded Jack of whoever it was who got the first chance that afternoon, but he refrained from sharing that with Pam.

"Don't worry, Pam! I'm going. Just get off your high horse."

+++

As Pam and Jack were getting ready for bed, she turned to him.

"Oh, I'm so excited about this trip I almost forgot something. You got a phone call today."

"A phone call? Here? Why didn't they call me at the office? Or was it personal?"

"He said he didn't want to bother you at work, but he wanted me to tell you something."

"What did he say?"

"He said he was calling on behalf of the Berium Corporation. Have you heard of it?"

Jack twitched just a little, then recomposed himself.

"I don't think so. Did he say anything else?"

"Just that he thought you and Bernie might be interested in investing in it. He told me to tell you to think about it for a few days and he'd call you back or stop by."

Pam thought Jack looked unnerved by what she told him.

"Is something wrong?"

"No. I think I know who the guy is now. He called me a couple of weeks ago about investing in some new company he was starting. I told him I wasn't interested, but he told me to think it over and he'd call me back. I bet that's who called you. He didn't leave his name, did he?"

"Yeah, he left his name and that of another guy. Let me get it. I wrote it down and put it in my purse. Yeah, here it is. He said when you call, either ask for Bob Cartwright or Vince Allred."

"You didn't tell him we were getting ready to leave on vacation, did you?"

"Of course not. You told me not to tell anyone."

"Well, maybe he'll find someone else while we're gone. I just know I'm not interested and I doubt if Bernie is, either. Now let's get some sleep. We have an early day tomorrow."

"Are you sure you're okay?"

"I told you I'm fine."

"Do you care if I Google the guy's company and check it out?"

"Pam, I don't want you messing in my business."

"But this isn't your business. Remember, you said you aren't interested."

"And I don't want you checking it out. You're liable to try to talk me into investing in this guy's scheme."

24

6

The First Day

The Archers packed that night, taking everything they thought either of them might want on a two-week vacation. They left at the scheduled time on Friday morning, headed a few miles down I-75 before they stopped somewhere for breakfast.

When they left the restaurant and got back on the interstate Pam noticed that Jack continued to check his rearview mirror.

"Trouble?"

"Huh? Oh, no. Just making sure there's no one back there."

Pam tried to turn around and look.

"Don't distract me. I can keep an eye on things. If I need your help I'll let you know."

An hour later they left Kentucky behind. Pam persuaded Jack to pull over at the Welcome Center so they could use the restroom and pick up some pamphlets.

"Take your time. I just need to make a couple of calls."

As Pam headed indoors Jack walked over to the deserted picnic area. He checked to make sure no one was around, then made his first call.

"Hey, Carla, this is Jack. Something came up and I won't be in for a few days. Everything's fine, but I just have something I need to do. I can't tell you any more than that, but I'll be in touch."

Carla tried to find out if something was wrong with his health and where Jack would be, but he told her he was fine as far as he knew, and he couldn't tell anyone where he was headed. She hung up, disappointed.

Jack's next call was to the detective he had hired.

"Got anything."

"Maybe. Your partner left work in a hurry this morning. Probably a little after 10:00. Do you think he knows you're gone?"

"Well, I didn't tell him."

Jack talked for a couple more minutes, then ended that call and made another one, to another detective of sorts, but no one answered.

"It's me. We just crossed over into Tennessee. I assume you're around here somewhere. I looked for you on the way down, but I didn't see you. You know where we're going to be. We'll get to the chalet this afternoon, and we have plans tonight. I'm not sure what we'll be doing after that."

Jack ended his third call and assessed his situation. He wasn't sure what side Carla was on, but he felt he knew about everyone else. He walked over to the Welcome Center building, looked around the parking lot, and checked to see if he recognized friend or foe. If someone was there who answered either description then that someone was doing a good job of not being recognized. Jack figured he was safe and turned to walk inside to see if Pam was ready to leave. He was anxious to get to the chalet.

+++

A Smoky Mountain Mystery

When Jack saw a sign welcoming them to Sevierville, he knew that they were getting close. He drove on, going immediately from Sevierville into Pigeon Forge. Pam craned her neck left and right, taking in as much of the small town as she could. Everything seemed to be one attraction after another. Jack looked at the time and asked Pam if she was hungry. She nodded and he looked for someplace to eat. Not being picky, he found something quickly and they stopped and ate a leisurely lunch. As they drove on, Pam continued to take in as much of the town as she could. It was like nothing she had seen before. A few minutes later, they left Pigeon Forge behind and drove through the beautiful wooded area between Pigeon Forge and Gatlinburg. It was quite a contrast to the small town they had just driven through. In Pigeon Forge, it seemed like everything was built to outdo the place next to it. Under the cover of trees, it looked like they had everything all to themselves. Well, they would have if it wasn't for all the other cars in front, in back, and beside them. The picturesque scenery ended too soon, and their tree covering gave way to the sky and another civilization full of buildings. Just before hitting the downtown area of Gatlinburg, they turned off to the left, onto East Parkway. Jack knew that once they left that road, there would be a lot of turns as they headed farther up into the mountains. He made sure that his map and his GPS agreed on the location of the chalet. A few minutes later Jack eased the Sequoia down a paved road mainly hidden by trees and pulled up in front of a chalet that appeared to be theirs for the next couple of weeks.

"Well, so far, so good. At least the part we can see doesn't look like some ramshackle lean-to that will be carried away by the next strong wind."

"It looks nice, at least on the outside."

"Well, let's get inside and see if the part we rented looks as good."

Twenty or so feet in front of them was the front door, located on the second level of the chalet. They each grabbed some luggage and headed toward the house. Jack adjusted what he carried, keyed in the security code, and pushed open the door. They walked down the hall and entered into a spacious living room, with a kitchen off to the right. But all they saw was what lay in front of them. The whole back wall was a window that looked out upon God's beauty. It looked even better because they were so high up in the mountains. Because their view was hidden from the road by the trees and the chalet, they had no idea what it was like until they stepped inside. They emptied their arms and embraced.

"Oh, Jack, this is wonderful. And I'm sorry if I've been a pain lately."

"Before you start getting all mushy on me, let me tell you the good news and the bad news."

"You mean we're only here for one night, and then we check into the place where the wind whistles through the cracks in the walls?"

"Nothing like that. It's just that I've planned our first two days here."

"Oh?"

"We're only here for a few minutes today, before heading out again. I've booked us for a show tonight that I thought you might like. Something called the Hatfield & McCoy Dinner Show. It's a comedy show with a meal included. They have two shows, but I've booked us for the first show. That means we can come back and take advantage of the hot tub. And if you remember correctly, I said that there are no other people nearby, if you get my drift."

Pam looked confused.

"What's the matter? You don't like the show or the hot tub?"

"I think I'm going to love both shows. It's just that you said good news and bad news. None of this sounds like bad news to me."

"The bad news is that there's some work I need to get finished before we enjoy our vacation, so tomorrow I'm sending you into Gatlinburg, or Pigeon Forge, your choice, to take in the place and shop to your heart's content. I don't want to see you until late afternoon. The reason we stopped by that little grocery on the way here is so I won't starve tomorrow, and we can eat dinner here tomorrow night. After that, I promise I'm all yours, except for an emergency, of course. Besides, this will allow you to check out Gatlinburg, and Pigeon Forge too if you like. But then you've already seen a drive-thru glimpse of Pigeon Forge, and you'll see most of it again tonight, at least a drive-thru example of it because that's where the Hatfield & McCoy show is. By the time you get back tomorrow, you might have more of an idea what you want to do over the next couple of weeks."

"Okay with me, as long as you promise you won't be working most of the time you're here. Now, let's check this place out before we leave it."

"Okay, let's check out the deck first. That's where the hot tub is."

Jack opened the door that led out onto the deck and motioned for Pam to go before him. To the right was a hot tub, covered for the time being. Straight ahead was a beautiful view that looked out onto the mountains in the distance. To the left was a table and some chairs, a good place to enjoy breakfast if the weather was right. Pam wrapped her arm around Jack, happier than she had been in some time. After a couple of minutes, he led her inside and showed her the master bedroom, which had a king-size bed and another spectacular view. Off it was the largest of three bathrooms. The others were on the other two levels.

The one on the top level was a full bath, with a half-bath on the bottom level.

"Let's hurry this along. Top or bottom first?"

"Huh?"

"Which level do you want to check out next?"

"Oh, let's go up."

When they arrived at the top level, they noticed an even more beautiful view, because it was above the trees and they could see for miles. On each end of that level was another bedroom, with a bathroom near the stairs in the middle. As Pam looked out at the panoramic view, she wondered if two weeks in the mountains were enough.

They trotted down the steps in single file, all the way to the bottom. They arrived and found a game room, with a pool table, a dartboard, a ping pong table, and a pinball machine. And if they so wished they would able to open a door and walk outside. Like the top two levels, this lower level had windows all across the back wall, with drapes to pull when you wanted some privacy. As if that mattered. From their vantage point and the proximity of any trails, roads, or cabins and chalets, no one could see them, even if that someone had a high-powered telescope.

+++

They left, got another quick glimpse of Pigeon Forge, only a little more crowded this time, and headed to the show, where they ate until they were full and laughed until their sides hurt. It was late when they returned to the chalet, but Pam made sure Jack had not forgotten his promise of the hot tub.

As she lay in bed that night, Pam thought, "*If this is what a vacation is like I don't want to wait so long for the next one.*"

7

The Second Day

People on vacation are usually friendly, and at the Hatfield & McCoy Show, Pam found herself talking to some of the other vacationing couples, both before and after the show. And she was happy she did. She found people who had made multiple trips to the area. Pam had read the brochures Jack brought home, and she had devoured the websites she checked out online, but there is something to be said for other people's experiences, so she listened to what each one had to say. She received suggestions on what to do and where to eat, as well as how different the towns of Gatlinburg and Pigeon Forge are laid out. She was told that most of the time there is available parking for the shows, restaurants, businesses, and attractions in Pigeon Forge, while she was wished good luck in finding a parking spot in Gatlinburg. She was told to arrive early and park on River Road, or find a parking lot because empty spots on the street were few and far between, and there are no parking spaces on the main street through town. Also, she was told that Gatlinburg is long and narrow, as the town is set in a valley, surrounded by mountains. And the best advice she received was to wear comfortable walking shoes, although she was told that the trolley might become her new best friend. She learned that each trolley route is a different color and runs to a different place, including a route that leads into the Smokies, and another route that runs from Gatlinburg to Pigeon Forge. But Pam was sure that staying in a secluded chalet meant that no trolley ran near there.

She thanked her new acquaintances for all their information. Some of it she had already acquired by reading up on the places, but much of it was new to her. And after they arrived, she learned that she would spend her first day in the Smokies alone.

+++

Pam Archer was the stay-at-home wife of a wealthy businessman, but she was no airhead. Pamela Ann Goodwin was the only child of Charles and Ruth Goodwin. Her parents married late in life and Ruth was thirty-seven years old when she had Pam. Pam grew up in a middle-class household, never wanting for anything, but she didn't have everything that some of the other girls had. When Pam was fourteen her dad died suddenly. He had saved some money and had a very good life insurance policy, so the family of two was able to carry on. Pam's mother had always insisted that Pam be a well-rounded person, so not only could she cook most any meal, but she could defend herself from most boys, knew a lot about most sports, and learned how to shoot a gun.

At age sixteen Pam took an after school job working in a drugstore. Pam's grades, which were mostly A's up to that point, fell to a mixture of A's and B's, but her mother didn't mind and felt her daughter needed some social time as well as school and work time. When she got to college, she took a part-time job in an office, and she worked full-time and worked her way up into management after she graduated.

A Smoky Mountain Mystery

Just before her twenty-eighth birthday, Pam met Jack Archer, and five months later they married. Pam's mother thought that they married too soon, that they didn't have enough time to get to know each other. But Pam was afraid that if she didn't marry Jack another man might not come along. She had been hoping for a husband ever since she turned twenty-one. When she and Jack married, he told her she should work for a year until they got on their feet, and then stay home. When Jack's business was doing well after a year of marriage, he reminded her of that and she quit her job. But she was still able to think for herself, and perfectly able to entertain herself on her first trip into Gatlinburg.

+++

Pam woke up excited on Saturday morning, eager to see what a vacation was like, only it wasn't starting the way she intended. But Jack had promised her his work would take only one day, so she agreed to check out her surroundings by herself.

Jack was still sleeping when she awoke, not long after sunrise, so she slipped out of bed quietly and headed to the shower. A few minutes later she stepped out of the shower and walked back to the bedroom to get dressed. She allowed herself a couple of minutes to ease over to the window and enjoy the early morning view. She couldn't believe how beautiful the area was.

Jack stirred as she finished dressing, but she could tell he wasn't fully awake. She kissed him on the cheek and he mumbled something that made a little sense.

The mountain air greeted her as she opened the door and headed to the Sequoia. As she did so, she spotted a squirrel scurrying up a tree with breakfast. Pam's stomach growled and she stepped up her pace. She sighed as she sat down in the driver's seat, hopeful that she wouldn't make any wrong turns on her way down the mountain. Once she made it to East Parkway, her turns got easier. One right turn and she was off to Gatlinburg. She had gotten a glimpse of Pigeon Forge the night before. Now she wanted to see what Gatlinburg was like. Not wanting to waste time or get lost, and with money being no object, once she got to town she pulled into the first parking lot she saw and hoped she didn't have to walk too far. Well, at least she remembered to wear comfortable walking shoes.

It didn't take her long to realize that the buildings that housed the businesses in Gatlinburg were smaller than the ones in Pigeon Forge, and most of them came all the way out to the sidewalk. She suspected that the town wasn't yet as crowded as it would be in a couple of hours. But people were milling about, some of the businesses were open, and traffic was moving up and down the street. although at a slow pace.

Pam was told that breakfast at Pancake Pantry was a must, and the best time to go was when they first open, or after 10:30. Breakfast is served the entire time they are open, and closing time varies from 3:00 to 4:00 p.m., depending upon the time of year. Most of the morning the line is out the door and meanders off in one direction or another. Well, Pam didn't make it by 7:00, when they opened, but she felt many of those frequenting the area were still in bed or getting ready to head out as she neared the restaurant. She looked up, spotted Pancake Pantry on the left. The line was out the door when she arrived, but there were only ten or so people ahead of her.

Pam had already learned that directions are given by traffic light numbers, not street names, and the lights are numbered 1-10. East Parkway enters Gatlinburg at Light 3. The Smoky Mountains are past Light 10. The main road through town is called the Parkway. And while attractions are leading off the Parkway at many of the traffic lights, the Parkway is where you find most people, most of the congestion, and most of what is worth seeing on the Parkway is between Lights 5-10. During peak season the cars on the Parkway resemble those driven by teenagers cruising a drive-in restaurant in days gone by. Traffic inches along, and everyone is there.

The Pancake Pantry is just past Light 6, which isn't far past Light 5. As Pam stood in line on her first morning in Gatlinburg, each time the door open smells wafted out of the restaurant. Those smells made her even hungrier.

A few minutes later she was seated and had ordered. After a few more minutes, she was a couple of bites into a plateful of chocolate chip pancakes, which was enough for Pam to realize that one trip to the Pancake Pantry wouldn't be enough. She couldn't wait to introduce Jack to the Pancake Pantry fare. The menu contained enough varieties of pancakes, crepes, and other breakfast fare that she and Jack wouldn't be in the area long enough to try everything on the menu.

Pam was adjusting to spending her first full day in the area alone. Only the two men who seemed to be watching her, without seeming to as they ate, unnerved her. Why were they interested in her? She didn't know either of them.

One of the men, who looked to be around her age, seemed merely curious, but the other man, who looked more like what she would call a thug, made her shudder. Was he watching her? Pam tried to watch both of them discretely. Neither of them seemed interested in anyone else in the place except Pam. She thought about calling Jack but remembered that he was working, and he would have a better chance of completing the work he had brought with him if he could do it undisturbed. Besides, a call to Jack would alarm him and he had no way of getting to her. And her fears abated when neither of the two men, who weren't seated together, followed her when she left the restaurant. Maybe it was just her imagination, after learning what Jack had shared with her about Bernie.

Bernie. It was the first time she had thought about him since she first cast her eyes on their chalet. She wondered if he meant harm to her husband, or were both partners afraid that the other one might get a little ahead of him. Pam dismissed any thoughts of Bernie and focused on enjoying her vacation.

Pam's agenda for the day was merely to walk from one end of the town to the other, scout out places she might want to explore later on, and if she was tired after all of her walking, she would take the trolley back to her car. She was surprised to see a McDonald's and a Wendy's among the small stores and shops located on the Parkway. Neither was on her list of places to visit before she left town, unless she saw no other suitable place to eat, or was in a hurry. At least there was no drive-thru at either place, so both did blend in somewhat with the rest of the facade. Most buildings were located right by the sidewalk, except for a few set-aside shopping areas. And there were a few large buildings of two or three floors, where you could go inside and find several stores. This was unlike Pigeon Forge where the thoroughfare was several lanes wide, and next came parking lots before people got to the attractions.

Pam noticed a lot of places that looked like there should be a barker out front urging people inside. She also did a quick perusal of shops that sold items she would be happy to have in her home, some costing hundreds of dollars. A few hours of walking and shopping made Pam realize that it was lunchtime. She stopped off at an odd-sounding place called Fanny Farkle's. She remembered that a couple of her newfound friends she met the night before had recommended a Fanny Farkle's sausage sub to her. The person in line in front of her ordered one, which consisted of a large sausage on a bun, topped with onions, peppers, and spices. She selected one, too, and was ready to see if her opinion was similar to that of the people she had met the night before. There were no tables, so she sat down on a nearby bench facing the shops while she ate and watched the vacationing world go by. She ate slowly, trying to complete her experience without making a mess. As she sat, eating and people-watching, she wondered if Gatlinburg was a town she would enjoy living in or one she would soon tire of. A few hours into her vacation, she had no idea which was true.

Pam finished eating and glanced at her watch. 1:30. She needed to give Jack a couple more hours before arriving back at the chalet, but that didn't mean that she needed to spend all that time in Gatlinburg. And she felt she didn't have enough time to check out the national park. Instead, she headed back to her car, planning to trust her map and her GPS and see some of the other cabins and chalets in the mountains. She was anxious to see how many of them she could find and how the others compared to the one her husband had rented.

Of course, she knew that some of them would be like the one Jack rented. One floor was below the area where they parked, so not only was their chalet larger than it looked from the front, but she didn't know until they went inside how well furnished it was. She was certain she wasn't sleeping on the same bed or sitting on the same couch, that others had done ten years before her. She wasn't even sure that her chalet was ten years old. It looked new.

8

Before leaving downtown Gatlinburg behind, Pam checked to see where she was compared to where the chalet was located. One trip up and down the mountainous terrain into town was not enough for her to be able to find her way back. It wasn't like they were staying on a mountain overlooking Gatlinburg. Coordinates showed that she was 8.2 miles from where they were staying. There were several mountain roads identified leading off the main road back, and she figured numerous other roads not marked. She didn't want to be more than one road away from one identified on her map, so she remained cautious. As she drove, she found a gated community and managed to talk her way inside, after she told the guard at the gate that she and her husband were thinking of buying a vacation home in the area. The place was exclusive enough that she had to wait while someone in the office did a quick credit check on Jack. Once they were certain that Pam's husband could afford to buy more than one home there if he so chose, they gave Pam a pass inside. She was even told where to go to see some chalets that were for sale. She was given the numbers of some that were open, where she could look around inside. She checked out a couple of them and was impressed. The view from the parapet on the top level at one of the homes surpassed the view where they were staying. And Pam couldn't get enough of that view.

A Smoky Mountain Mystery

After staying a half hour or so and leaving with literature she could show Jack, she chose another road and drove off to see what it had to offer. She made one wrong turn and ended up on a dead-end gravel road, and after one more wrong turn, she found a cabin she could barely see back in the woods. She saw no one around, so she got out, stretched her legs, and took her camera to shoot a few pictures. As it turned out, the cabin, which appeared to be deserted, resembled the one she had been afraid would be theirs for two weeks. She even tried the front door and found out it was unlocked. She heard or saw no one, but decided that two minutes in a place like that were enough.

She found her way back to a road she recognized on her map, and checked out two other roads, with picturesque views. She stopped the SUV, got out, and took a few more shots with her camera. She heard a noise, saw a squirrel scamper across the road and up a tree and a rabbit bound off in another direction, but both were too fast for her to catch them with her camera. Another noise alerted her that there were two bear cubs nearby, the first bears she had seen outside of a zoo. She also knew enough about bear cubs to know that momma was somewhere nearby, and Pam didn't want to reenact a more violent version of Goldilocks and the Three Bears. She quickly put her camera away, got into her vehicle, and drove away.

After turning off from one road to another, she spotted another SUV not far behind her. As far as she could tell, it had tinted windows. She had no interest in meeting new friends, or enemies, so far away from her husband and civilization, so off she sped, taking first one road and then another. When she felt she had lost the other vehicle, she checked her phone and saw it was time to head back to her husband. She had gone a little out of her way to lose her tail if she had one, but consulted her GPS and took the quickest route home. Just after she turned down the road leading to the chalet Jack had rented, she rounded a curve

and spotted an SUV that might have been the one following her earlier. At least it looked similar and had tinted
windows. She gasped, hit the gas and zipped around the
other vehicle, and charged ahead to check on Jack. She
stopped in front of the chalet, noted that the other vehicle
hadn't turned around to follow her, and rushed inside to
make sure that her husband was okay.

+++

"Finished working?"

"You've got good timing. I just finished five minutes
ago. So, did you have a good time without me?"

"Not as good as I would have had with you."

"You don't know that. So, where did you go and what
did you do?"

"I'll fill you in later. Has anyone been here?"

"No. Why? You seem like something's bothering you.
Did you see someone?"

"Well, just after I turned to come up this way, I
passed another SUV coming from this direction."

"From what I understand there's nothing else this
way. What did it look like?"

"Large, dark color, American made."

"Could you tell who was inside?"

"No, it had tinted windows."

"Well, maybe it was someone who was lost."

"I'm not sure, but I think it was the same vehicle I
saw earlier today. All I know for sure is that the other one
was an SUV and it had tinted windows."

Jack went over to the table, opened a drawer, and
took out a gun.

"Where did you get that?"

"I bought it a couple of weeks ago. The guy I hired
recommended I get one."

"You know how I feel about guns."

"And you probably know how I'd feel about getting shot. I feel better knowing I have some sort of protection."

"When were you going to tell me that you bought a gun?"

"I wasn't unless it became necessary. I didn't want you to worry. But enough about that. I finished what I was working on. Now we can relax and enjoy a nice dinner. I got steaks, and this place has a grill."

"Does this place have an alarm system?"

"I'm not sure."

"I think it's time you become sure."

+++

An hour or so later, after no one had burst through the door with bullets flying, Pam had calmed down enough to resume thinking about their vacation.

"So, darling, did you have a good time today?"

"It would have been more fun with you, but yeah, I enjoyed myself."

"And will I enjoy looking at the credit card bill?"

"I didn't buy anything. Yet. Just meals, and some delicious donuts and fudge we can snack on if we get hungry."

"So what do you want to do tomorrow?"

"I don't know. What are you up for?"

"I don't know. I thought it might be nice to take a picnic lunch and check out the national park. That Cade's Cove place sounds nice. Then, before we come back here tomorrow, we can stop off in town and enjoy a good dinner."

"All that sounds good to me, and it will be better than today because we'll be together."

Pam waited for her husband to agree, but he didn't say anything.

9

The Third Day

Pam awoke the next morning and lay there looking up through the window at the sun filtering in through the trees. There was something to be said for being out away from it all and enjoying God's creation. She lay there a moment, then shifted her eyes to the ceiling, beautiful wood, just like the rest of the interior of the chalet. She smiled and thought back to the time they had spent in the hot tub the night before. She didn't know why they had never bought one for their home. Her thoughts turned to Jack and she rolled over to put her arm around her husband, but he wasn't there.

"Jack?"

No answer.

"Jack!"

Pam tossed the covers aside and sprang from the bed, to search for her husband. She headed through the doorway, frantically looking this way and that, until she spotted him through the window, standing outside, talking on his cell phone. She hurried toward the door, but when he heard her coming, he turned and stuck his hand up, like a policeman stopping traffic. At least he was okay, so she remained inside, but started pacing, impatiently waiting for her husband to end his call. Who was he talking to? Was it work again?

A couple of minutes later Jack opened the door, looked at his wife, and smiled.

"Who were you talking to?"

"It was the guy I hired. I felt it was best if I told him about the SUV you saw yesterday, just in case it meant anything. It probably doesn't, but it pays to be cautious."

"I was worried about you when I woke up and you weren't there."

"I'm armed. Remember? Now, let's forget about it. What do you want to do about breakfast?"

"I found this great place yesterday you'd probably like. That is if you want to stop and take time to eat before we head to the Smokies. We are still going, aren't we?"

"Of course, and I'd be glad to check out this breakfast place you found. Let's hop in the shower, then pack a picnic lunch, and head to town."

+++

Sunday morning's line to get into the Pancake Pantry was longer than the day before, but the Wildberry Crepes that Pam ordered melted in her mouth. The crepes were loaded with five different berries and a mixture of cream and ricotta cheeses, sprinkled with powdered sugar and topped with real whipped cream. Jack passed on Pam's selection but enjoyed his ham and hash brown omelet and three buttermilk pancakes as much as Pam enjoyed her choice.

"I'm not sure I'll be ready for lunch anytime soon, but I'm glad you found this place. Now I know why it's crowded. It's hard to keep places like this a secret."

"I'm glad those people I met the other night shared their secret with me. There are so many restaurants around here with the name Pancake. I don't see how any of the others could be this good. Maybe we can come back down here sometime just for the weekend."

"Hey, we just got here. Don't go wishing away this vacation."

"Oh, don't worry. I'm excited about the next thirteen days."

Pam looked around. The place was crowded but the set-up of the restaurant allowed her to see quite a few of the tables. There was no sign of either of the men she had seen the morning before. Maybe they were just vacationers who had no idea who she was and didn't care where she went when she left, or who she was with. But they sure did seem interested in her, and one of them looked like a guy she wouldn't want to see if she left the Parkway.

When Jack and Pam walked out of the restaurant, both of them noticed that there was still a line to get in.

"Look at that line. Either your friends are spending all their vacation telling people about this place, or a lot of other people are doing the same."

"And I hear the line is even longer earlier in the morning. Of course, they say the line is longer on the week-end."

"Then I say let's come back during the week."

"My guess is there's a line then, too. So, is there anything we need to pick up here in town before we head off to the park and our picnic?"

"Not unless you can think of something."

"No, it looks like you were thorough when you packed the picnic basket."

+++

The two of them headed back to the SUV, unaware that someone was watching them from across the street, in the direction away from where they were walking. A few blocks later, Jack clicked his key and opened the vehicle.

A Smoky Mountain Mystery

He and Pam got in and sat down. Pam turned to make sure the picnic basket her husband had found inside the chalet was where they had left it. It reminded her of how thoughtful the people who own the chalets are. Most anything they could have possibly wanted could be found inside the cabin, including plates, glasses, silverware, and brand new bottles of condiments.

The traffic wasn't yet what it would become later in the day. Maybe some of the locals, and vacationers too went to church first and would take in the national park in the afternoon. At any rate, traffic wasn't as heavy as it would be in peak time, so in a matter of minutes, they had left Gatlinburg behind and were on their way to the Great Smoky Mountain National Park. Pam remembered to bring her camera along, and she planned to ask Jack to pull over anytime she felt there was a scene she wanted to capture and take home with her, provided there was someplace he could pull off the road and let her get out.

A few minutes later, they passed the sign welcoming them to the national park, and were on the road that dissected the park and would take them to Cherokee, North Carolina, provided they wanted to go that far. They wouldn't come close to Cherokee. At least not on that day, because the right turn headed up the mountain to Cade's Cove would come well before they left the state of Tennessee behind.

"There it is," Pam said, and turned and smiled at her husband.

"I see it."

A sign posted beside the road alerted them that Cade's Cove was the next right turn, and once they turned, another sign let them know that it was farther to Cade's Cove than Pam had realized.

"Wow! This park must be larger than I thought. I figured it wouldn't be more than five miles to anywhere in the park. It's certainly farther than that to Cade's Cove. It's like twenty miles from here. And the park is a lot bigger than that."

"There's nothing like this around Lexington. That's for sure."

Pam looked at the side mirror and noticed the line of cars following them. While one of the vehicles was an SUV, it didn't have tinted windows. She breathed a sigh of relief.

The beautiful scenery improved when something she called a stream, but the locals called Little Pigeon River, headed up the mountain beside them. It wasn't the first time she'd seen the narrow river. It ran through Pigeon Forge, and River Road in Gatlinburg was so named because the Little Pigeon River flowed beside it. In most places, the water was so shallow that they could see the rocks in the river. Someone might get his head bashed on the rocks, but there was no way he was going to drown. At least not in any part of the river that Pam had seen. A couple of times along the way she noticed young people frolicking as they rode inner tubes down the river. Other times the water was so low that the tubes had to be carried over the rocks to the next good place to put them back into the water.

Several miles later, the Archers reached the beginning of the Cade's Cove Trail Loop. There was a large parking lot, and a welcome center of sorts, for anyone who wanted to stop. Jack turned to her and she sensed his question.

"On you huskies."

Neither of them could believe how flat the land was on top of the mountain, and that there was a huge parcel of land void of trees. There was flat land so large that the best of the major league sluggers couldn't possibly hit a baseball from one end of it to the other. From reading the material that was sent to them, and from what they learned on the Internet, there were several points of interest along the Cade's Cove Loop. The first was an old cabin, a quarter of a mile walk from the nearest parking area.

"Let's check it out," Pam said, so Jack pulled in and took one of the available parking places. There were two ways of getting back to the cabin. One was through the trees, although it wasn't a heavily wooded area, and the other was through a field.

"Let's go through the trees, and come back across the field."

"Sounds okay to me. And it's too early for us to picnic, so grab your camera and let's check this place out."

"You seem to be enjoying this trip."

"Well, at least the chalet, that breakfast place, and the park. I've been so busy working that I'd forgotten that places like this still exist."

"I know. It does you good to get away now and then. Jack, it doesn't always have to be here, but we need to get away somewhere every few months."

The two stepped over an occasional fallen log and continued up the trail until they arrived at the cabin. Pam got her camera out and sent Jack ahead so she could take a picture of him standing in front of the cabin. There were a few other travelers around, as well as a National Park Service employee there to answer any questions anyone might have.

"This would be a good place to have a picnic."

"Yeah, if it wasn't so early and just an hour and a half or so since we had that large scrumptious breakfast."

"Do you have any ideas for our picnic spot from looking at that map of yours?"

"You can't tell much what each place looks like, only where it is. I'd say we wait until we see the bears, and then we can get the picnic basket out."

"Yeah, right! Somehow I don't think these bears are named Yogi and Boo Boo."

"Okay, we'll forget the bears. But three of the places along here are churches. Maybe we can stop at one of them and eat."

"Why? Are they having a potluck, or do they call them covered dish suppers down here?"

The two of them continued to take in their surroundings as they talked, even noticed a couple of riders on horseback.

"I didn't know you could ride horses up here."

"They even close this place off to cars a couple of mornings a week, so people can ride the loop on their bicycles."

"You're not getting me on a bicycle."

"How about a horse?"

"I think I'll pass on that one, too."

Jack checked his phone, saw that it was almost noon.

"Hey, we'd better get moving unless we want to be here past dark. And that won't happen because they close the road before dark."

"Yeah, but they say early and late in the day is the best time to see a bear."

"That's another good reason to be gone before dark."

+++

Jack and Pam continued their journey around the oval roadway, stopping at an occasional point of interest, but when their stomachs started growling as they got to the Primitive Baptist Church, the third church on the loop, they stopped to have their picnic. More than likely most people had already seen most of the places that interested them because only two other cars stopped to check out the church during the whole time the Archers were there. They enjoyed various gourmet cheeses, crackers, and a few other treats with a chilled bottle of wine, something neither of them drank often.

A Smoky Mountain Mystery

It was mid-afternoon when they arrived at the spot with the most places to park, the most attractions to see without getting back into their SUV, and the most cars they had seen since they arrived at Cade's Cove. Places to see included a working grist mill, a corn crib, a smokehouse, a barn, a blacksmith shop, a place to buy postcards and other things, and restroom facilities. They decided to begin at the grist mill and work their way back to the small building that sold souvenirs, then hit the restrooms before heading back to the car. The grist mill fascinated Pam, so she and Jack lingered there a while and listened to what the man had to say. She contemplated buying some of the cornmeal when they checked out the store before leaving.

Jack hadn't shown any sign that he was in a hurry, and they weren't on a set schedule, so Pam strolled along, looking this way and that, stopping from time to time to capture a photograph. They passed one small building and then another, and stopped occasionally to enjoy the shade provided from the trees, and eventually arrived at the small store.

There were a few things to eat, and lots of items for sale that proved that someone had been to the Great Smoky Mountain National Park. After both of them had seen all there was to see, Pam walked toward the front door while Jack got in line to pay for their purchases.

10

Pam had stepped out onto the porch and was looking around to see what she could see when she saw a familiar face walking past her, coming from the direction of the men's restroom. It was one of the two men she had seen at Pancake Pantry when she'd eaten breakfast there on Saturday morning, the one who looked the surliest of the two. Had the man seen them in Gatlinburg and followed them to Cade's Cove? Once they headed into the Smokies he wouldn't have to remain right behind them. And once they turned right and headed up the mountain to Cade's Cove, the odds were over ninety percent as to where they were headed. He could have remained back, or even surged ahead of them when they stopped at the cabin or one of the churches. Whatever the case, the sight of him was enough to ruin Pam's day, or at least make it less appealing.

She gasped for breath, unsure whether to rush back inside and tell her husband or not. She decided to remain on the porch and see if she could tell where the man was headed. From her vantage point on the porch, only slightly higher than the parking lot but with a clear view, she could see that he had walked almost to the other end of the parking lot. He got into an SUV, that appeared to have tinted windows. And then he just sat there. Was there someone else with him? He was alone when she saw him on Saturday, but he might have picked up a partner somewhere along the line.

A few seconds later Jack walked out and tapped Pam on the shoulder. She jumped.

"Hey, what's the matter? Jumpy all of a sudden."

She grabbed him by the arm and pulled him around to the side of the building, where they couldn't be overheard.

"What's wrong?"

"That man. I saw him just now."

"What man? You didn't say anything about any man. You mean the one that was near the place we rented?"

"I don't know about that. Remember, the windows were tinted. But he got in an SUV just now, and I think it has tinted windows. Anyway, it's the man I saw at Pancake Pantry."

"What man? Why didn't you tell me at the time?"

"I didn't see him there today. This was yesterday. He was one of two suspicious men I saw there yesterday."

"Are you sure you weren't on edge because of what I told you before you left?"

"I don't know. But he looked suspicious then, and he still does today. Let's go confront him."

"Wait a minute! I don't have my gun. I left it back in the cabin. Let's just drive by and get the license number. I can have my guy check it out."

They hurried to their vehicle, which was parked much closer to where they were than the one the man had gotten into.

"Okay. I'm going to drive out of here. When we get close, point out where he is. Is his car on the left or the right?"

"This side. The left. But a lot closer to the other end of the parking area."

Jack pulled out slowly and eased toward the other end of the lot. No other vehicles pulled out in front or behind him.

"There. Heck, he's gone. He was where that vacant space is now."

"Are you sure he was the same guy you saw yesterday?"

"I think so. He looked the same. And he's following us."

"First of all, he's not following us now. He left before we did. Keep an eye out and see if we see him on the way out. We still can't go but 15 miles per hour, because that's the limit for this place, but he might pull over somewhere and try to get behind us again. Provided there really is a guy stalking us, or one of us."

They didn't need to worry about exceeding the speed limit. It was almost 5:00 and a lot of people were leaving the park, heading back to a cabin or a motel room, even though there was still plenty of daylight left.

They drove for a while, and then they noticed that the traffic ahead of them had stopped.

"What's wrong, Jack?"

"I don't know that anything's wrong. Maybe it's especially scenic ahead and someone stopped to take some pictures. You might try taking some. It might take your mind off this guy."

"Well, I'd feel better if you'd brought your gun. I bet he has his."

"I can see the headline now. Shootout at Smoky Mountain National Park."

"Just be careful."

"I am."

A hundred or so feet ahead of them, Jack pointed out why everyone was stopping. There were deer near the road, eating at the grass just on the other side of a fence, not paying any attention to the people driving by. And over in a meadow behind them, Jack pointed to a wild turkey.

The meadow was on the left, but less than a quarter of a mile ahead on the right traffic slowed again, and Jack and Pam noticed another deer, this one meandering through the trees on the right.

"Disappointed you haven't seen a bear?"

"I've already been scared once today. Once is enough. Let's save the bear for the next time, and hopefully, it isn't as close as these deer."

Jack drove on and the pace picked up. The deer had headed deeper into the trees. Neither of them saw anyone suspicious on the rest of the loop road, or on the way back down the mountain and out of the park.

+++

Pam relaxed slightly as they left the national park behind.

"Are we still going to Best Italian to eat?"

"Of course! We're not going to let someone ruin our vacation. I know how much you've been looking forward to this. Besides, he hasn't threatened you, has he?"

"No, he just looked suspicious."

"I bet most people see a lot of suspicious people when they're on vacation."

"But this guy looked the part. He could play the heavy in a good movie."

"Only if he can act."

+++

Pam reminded Jack that there were two Best Italian restaurants in Gatlinburg. One was at Light 9, before they hit the main part of town, coming from the park. What someone had told her at the Hatfield's & McCoy show was that there was a little parking there. They might get lucky and not have to pay to park again. Not that a fee to park would make Jack change his lifestyle. It was more the convenience of the thing.

A couple of minutes later they found the restaurant. Unlike many of the small buildings in the area, it set back off the street, and its strip mall look didn't look nearly as impressive on the outside as Pancake Pantry did. The wood and glass of the Pancake Pantry's exterior matched the equally impressive food inside, and the shops nearby. Pam had even taken a picture of it. But not here. There was nothing special about this place. Well, not on the outside.

Jack parked. They got out, looked at the restaurant, and then each other. Both of them shrugged. Too many people had told Pam that the restaurant was well worth a visit for her to change her mind after only seeing the outside. There was nothing all that impressive about the inside either until the first of their food was set upon the table.

They chose an appetizer and a salad and enjoyed those while awaiting their entrees, both of which came with three garlic rolls swimming in butter, which someone had told Pam was worth the trip to the restaurant all by itself. Pam looked at the large portions and wondered how she was going to eat all that was set before her, but Jack quickly eased her mind.

"Well, it looks like we both have enough for tomorrow night, too."

"You can say that again."

"It looks like we both have enough for tomorrow night, too."

Pam smiled at Jack's retort and playfully swiped at him. The two enjoyed a leisurely dinner, not talking much, but smiling at each other occasionally. Both of them seemed to be preoccupied, thinking of something else. Finally, Jack broke the silence.

"So, do you want to walk around, show me some of this place, or would you rather go back to the chalet and relax?"

"I'm too full to walk, but after a ride back I could be coerced into spending some more time with you in the hot tub."

"I think we can arrange that."

+++

The delicious dinner and thoughts of spending time with her husband were enough to cause Pam to forget about the man in the SUV with the tinted windows. Well, forget about him unless he showed up again before the night was over.

+++

After relaxing in the hot tub, but before heading to bed for the night, the two of them agreed to spend the next day at the cabin. Sleep late, cook breakfast, maybe shoot a game of pool, and if the weather was good, and it was supposed to be, they could walk a couple of trails they had spotted from the top level of the chalet.

11

The Fourth Day

The next morning the two of them slept late, ate breakfast out on the deck, and went for a walk on one of the hiking trails nearby, before relaxing in the hot tub and taking a shower. Everything went well until Pam made a run to a small grocery not far away to pick up a couple of things to go with dinner.

"You sure you don't want me to go?"

"No, I'll be fine. I know where it is. You just enjoy yourself and I'll be back before you know it."

Pam left before Jack could argue. She wasn't sure why she felt compelled to go to the grocery, but a few minutes later she was glad she wasn't with her husband.

She picked up a few things at the grocery and was on her way back to the chalet when her phone rang. She hoped it wasn't Jack asking her to pick up something else. She was almost halfway back to where they were staying and didn't want to turn around and go back.

Pam looked to see who was calling and was surprised to see that the number was blocked. She looked in her rear-view mirror and saw that no one was following her, so she took the call.

"Is this Mrs. Archer?"

"Yes. Who's calling, please?"

"My name is Johnny Cairo. I'm a private detective hired by your mother. Are you where you can talk?"

The name Johnny Cairo immediately brought to mind the character Joel Cairo, played by Peter Lorre in *The Maltese Falcon*. At least the man didn't sound like Lorre, and probably didn't look as creepy. Pam shook her head to remove any thoughts of Lorre and turned her thoughts to the caller. She saw a place to pull over, checked the rearview mirror again to make sure no one was following her and decided to give the man her undivided attention.

"Okay, Mr. Cairo. What's wrong with my mother?"

"Nothing. It's just that she was concerned about your safety and hired me to see if you are as safe as you think you are."

"And am I?"

"I don't think so."

"Is it one of those men I saw the other day, or the man who's been following me in an SUV with tinted windows?"

"It might be. I'm not that far along yet, but I suspect that your husband might be planning to murder you. I shared this with your mother, and she asked me to call you."

"My husband? Murder me? We're on vacation. We're having the time of our lives."

"Sometimes a vacation is the best time to commit murder. No one knows you, and the victim is more likely to let his or her guard down while on vacation. Anyway, I already knew you're on vacation. I've managed to track you."

"How?"

"I have my ways. Did I mention I'm a private detective?"

"You did. And you also mentioned that you think my husband is planning to murder me. What makes you think that? Besides, he could have drowned me in the hot tub either of the last two nights. And I'm still here."

"And if he had done that, who would the police have suspected of your murder?"

"Okay. I'm listening. What do you have to say, and what makes you think he's trying to murder me?"

"Your mother has been suspicious for quite some time."

"My mother is always suspicious. She didn't want me to marry Jack. And it's not like he's after my money. He's the one with all the money."

"But maybe he doesn't want you around anymore and he doesn't want to share all that money if he divorces you."

"Go on."

"Well, I managed to get close enough to your husband when he didn't suspect anyone was eavesdropping. He was talking to another man about murder, and your name came up. But then so did his partner's. I couldn't hear all of what he said, but he did say something about trying to get it all. I assume he thinks you want all of his money."

"Maybe you misunderstood. As you said, you didn't hear it all. Maybe it's his partner who wants it all. I know theirs is not the best of relationships."

"You could be right. But do you know he purchased a gun recently?"

"I do."

"I can understand why he told you about it because I don't think he plans to shoot you. Too easy to determine guilt. He might have hired this man to kill you. You said something about a couple of men and an SUV with tinted windows. Maybe he plans for someone to murder you while you're on vacation."

"But he wouldn't have an alibi."

"I know. That's what bothers me. I think he plans to wait until he has an alibi, and then call the guy to come after you. Do you want me to come down there and keep an eye on you?"

"No. I can handle myself. I took a self-defense course a while back. I disarmed a man and put him on the floor, and he was twice my size."

"But I bet he wasn't twenty yards away carrying a gun."

"No, but I can shoot a gun, too. I took a course in that, too."

"It seems like you have some idea of how to protect yourself. But tell me, by any chance has your husband been showing you more attention recently, being nicer than normal?"

"He has, but I attribute that to the fact that we're on vacation."

"It could be because he doesn't want you to become suspicious."

"Okay, I'll keep my eyes open. Thanks for calling."

"Well, I just wanted to alert you. That's why your mother paid me. And if you change your mind, get in touch with your mother. She knows how to get in touch with me."

+++

Pam sat there, stunned. Did Jack want her out of the way? If so, why? Was there another woman? She checked again, but there was no other vehicle in sight. Neither Johnny Cairo nor a man driving an SUV with tinted windows, who could be the same person, appeared to be following her. Still, she didn't know what to do.

First, before she took off, she would call her mother, see if this guy Johnny Cairo was for real. The name sounded made up.

"Hello. Grace Abner here."

"And Pamela Grace Abner Archer here."

"Yeah, it's that last name that scares me."

"And that's why I called. Did you hire some guy named Johnny Cairo to see if Jack is trying to kill me?"

"Doesn't he have such a cute name?"

"So, I guess that's your way of saying 'yes'?"

"I don't trust Jack. Never did. And I think he has a girlfriend. Probably that girl at his office. They seem too close if you ask me."

"You've never even been to the office, and I don't believe anyone asked you. And I don't think the two of them have anything going on. I know they don't right now. Jack and I are in Gatlinburg."

"Gatlinburg? You went to Gatlinburg with that fiend without telling me?"

"No, I went with my husband without telling anyone. He's having some problems at work."

"I'll say. He can't figure out a way to get rid of his wife so he can marry his secretary. Honey, I'm worried about you."

"I figured that otherwise, you wouldn't spend your money hiring a detective."

"And did that detective tell you that he heard Jack talking to someone on the phone and that your name came up, and the word murder?"

"He did."

'And you're not concerned?"

"Of course it unnerved me, Mom. Something like that has to shake up anyone who has half a brain."

"I remember when you had a whole brain. It was sometime before you married."

"Don't worry, Mom. Feel free to keep in touch, but I can take care of myself."

The two ended the call, but Pam wondered about her last words. Could she take care of herself? Had Jack hired someone to kill her? Was he planning to murder her himself, or was all of this someone's vivid imagination?

With the first two possibilities, Pam wondered if she should be more worried if she was with her husband or if she was alone. She wasn't thinking clearly, but she needed to get back to Jack, so he wouldn't suspect anything.

12

Jack was on the phone when Pam returned. He looked up and saw her.

"I've got to go. Pam's back."

"Who was that?"

"Carla."

"Why did she call?"

"She didn't. I called her. She asked me to check in every couple of days, whenever it was convenient, just in case something came up that I needed to know about."

"And did anything come up?"

"No. Things seem to be going fine. That's if I can believe her. She doesn't appear to be Bernie's girl, but I'm not taking any chances. So, what's wrong with you, and what took you so long to get back?"

"Nothing's wrong."

"Pam."

"Okay, I talked to my mom while I was out. I'm worried about her. She seems to be getting more forgetful every time I talk to her."

"I wish she'd forget me."

"Jack."

"You know she doesn't like me."

"I wouldn't say that."

"I know you won't say it, but you know it. Anyway, there's nothing wrong with your mom. Now, are you ready to eat? Dinner's almost ready."

Pam tried to put her suspicions of Jack out of her mind but wasn't able to do so. Somehow she had to make Jack think that her only concern was about her mother's health, not her own.

+++

Neither of them spoke during dinner until Jack broke the silence just before they finished.

"Look. I can tell that something's bothering you. How about you and I go for a drive after dinner?"

"A drive? Why?"

"Why not? I thought it might take your mind off your troubles, whatever they are. We won't go far. Just around the mountains. Maybe stop somewhere and check out a scenic overlook or two."

Pam's mind was racing. She was having thoughts she didn't want to have, but thoughts that might solve her dilemma for a short time.

"Pam?"

"Oh, yeah, sure, Jack. Only how about you let me drive, and let me show you this place I stumbled upon yesterday?"

"You don't trust my driving? Yeah, okay, whatever you say. You can drive. Maybe it will take your mind off of what's troubling you."

+++

Neither of them paid any attention to the beautiful mountain scenery, evergreens interspersed with deciduous trees, an occasional break in the tree line with a view of the next ridge, or the smell of the mountain air. Neither looked for scampering squirrels or babbling brooks. Their minds were on other things.

Jack kept an eye on the speedometer and glanced at his wife from time to time. It wasn't that she was driving erratically. It was more the opposite. She was driving slower than usual, even allowing for the curvy mountain road, and she kept looking in the rearview mirror as if she was expecting company. Each time she did, Jack glanced in his side mirror, but there was nothing there, except for the beautiful mountainside they both had ignored. It was like the rest of the world had gone away and left the mountains to the two of them.

"It's beautiful up here, isn't it?"

"Uh...oh, yeah. It sure is."

"Listen. I don't know who or what you saw when you were out earlier, but you're not the same person you were this afternoon. Now, why don't you tell me about it? Maybe I can help you."

"I told you. It's Mom. I'm just worried about her is all."

"Listen, the last time I saw your mother she was the same suspicious self she has been any other time I've seen her. I don't think you have anything to worry about when it comes to your mother. She's liable to outlive both of us."

Pam jumped at Jack's latest statement.

"Look, there's a scenic overlook just ahead on the right. Why don't we take a few minutes to enjoy the view and then we can go see your place after that?"

"It'll be dark soon."

"That's why we should look at it now. Enjoy the sunset. Imagine we're back in the hot tub looking at the sun going down."

"We can't see the sunset from the hot tub, only from the top level."

"I meant to use your imagination."

"Why don't you use your imagination? I'll take you to the place I discovered, and then you can imagine you are sitting in a hot tub enjoying an overlook while we're there."

"Fine. We'll do it your way, but if you don't get back to your old self soon, I'm ready to go home."

"Just be quiet while I try to find this place."

13

Pam tried to recall where she had seen what looked like an abandoned cabin when she had stumbled upon it the day before. At times she came to a fork in the road, stopped, looked both ways, and pictured it in her mind before choosing her direction. Her unsure manner gave Jack doubts that she could find the place again, but he wasn't going to open his mouth. But Pam's method worked. A little under a half-hour later she spotted the dilapidated cabin just up ahead on their left. She pulled up to it, stopped, and sighed.

"Well, we're here."

"What? this run-down place? This was what you wanted to show me?"

"Sort of. What I want you to see is inside."

"Is that where they keep their rat collection? Okay. Let's go inside. Lead the way."

The two of them got out, shut the doors. The closing of the doors sounded so loud in the stillness of the mountains. Pam looked nervous and tried to keep her distance from her husband. She looked around to see if anyone was about. Even the animals seemed to have abandoned the place, so she and Jack could have it all to themselves.

Pam walked around the SUV to where Jack was, tried to smile, and put him at ease. He motioned for her to lead. That wasn't what she wanted. She wanted him to lead.

"No, guys first."

Jack nodded, not wanting to argue with his wife. He walked up the path toward the ramshackle cabin that looked like it hadn't been occupied in quite some time. It would take some kind of realtor to find the words to rent this eyesore.

Jack stopped in front of the cabin and turned to his wife.

"I said inside. Just climb the steps and open the door."

Jack nodded and started up the three steps to the small porch. He stopped and waited on his wife, who seemed to be more nervous than he was, then reached for the knob to open the door. Once he turned his head, Pam sprang into action. She reached into her pocket, opened a bottle of ether and drenched a cloth with it. Then, she reached up to an unsuspecting Jack and covered his mouth and nose with it. Jack was too surprised to struggle, and before he could do anything he stumbled against the partially opened door and fell to the floor, half in, half out of the cabin.

Pam looked around, made sure no one was rushing toward them. From what she could tell, her husband had no accomplices in the immediate area. She made sure the ether had served its purpose, then pulled Jack the rest of the way into the cabin and rushed back to the SUV. In the back of the vehicle were some items they carried in case of an emergency. She rummaged through the box, found some duct tape and scissors and ripped them from the box. When she returned, Jack looked the same as when she left him. She spotted a sink in the corner, with a pipe running down from the ceiling to a countertop. She dragged Jack over to it, lifted him to his feet, and leaned him against the sink while using her body to see that he didn't fall. All of this took all the energy she had. Her nervousness had sapped much of it.

Not only had Pam purchased ether after taking a class on protecting herself from a mugger, but she bought a pair of handcuffs, too. She slapped one handcuff on a large pipe that ran from the floor to the ceiling, and the other one on Jack's left wrist and snapped it in place. She used duct tape to secure Jack's feet to the pipe under the sink. Then she stood up and turned on the faucet. Surprisingly, it worked. That way Jack would have water to drink, once he awakened. She ran back once more to the SUV and grabbed a few packages of cheese and peanut butter crackers for Jack to eat. Her intent wasn't to kill Jack, just keep him where she knew where he was while she took time to think about what she planned to do. She checked Jack's pockets, made sure he didn't have a knife, then grabbed his cell phone. Jack was still out, but she wasn't sure how much longer that would be the case.

Pam looked out the partially open door. It was almost dark and she wanted to find her way back to the chalet without getting lost in the darkness. Besides, she wasn't sure if someone was out there somewhere looking for her. She didn't want to run into someone while she was out and about.

She hurried back to the SUV, got in, sat there for a moment, heaving and sobbing.

What had she done? Had what she had done saved her life, or hurt an innocent man and destroyed her marriage?

Pam started the vehicle, stepped on the gas, and headed back to the chalet, where she could think. If she could think rationally.

If anyone was following her, they were doing so without the aid of headlights. It was dark by the time she got back to the chalet. Pam looked in every direction. There appeared to be no other vehicles nearby. She got out, clicked the lock for the SUV, and hurried to the front door. She keyed in the code, opened the door, and pushed it back to make sure that no one was behind it. Cautiously she entered and turned on each light as she came to a new room, then hurried to find Jack's gun. She planned to sleep with it.

She didn't have a plan. She hadn't planned to do anything to Jack when she left. What should she do? Get out of there? She eliminated that possibility, knowing that she couldn't do that without going to get Jack, or leaving him there where more than likely no one would be able to find him. Eventually, that would make her a murderer. Should she leave him there until the next day, or the day after, then go back to the cabin and try to talk some sense into him? Tell him she was letting him go, but if he was planning to kill her, let him know that she would kill him first if it even looked like he was planning to do away with her.

But what if Jack was innocent? But then he couldn't be, could he? After all, her mother's private detective had heard Jack talking to some other guy about murdering her. Or was he planning to murder Bernie instead? Or was the detective confused, and what Jack had talked about was that Bernie was planning to murder him?

She thought about her predicament for a few minutes, but even then she had no more of an idea of what she should do. And then she thought of the police. Should she contact them and tell them that a private detective overheard Jack tell someone he wanted her dead? But would they believe her? And would they arrest her for what she had done to Jack? Should she play this as if nothing had happened? Or should she call the police and tell them she went somewhere and when she returned her husband was gone? She thought she knew what they would tell her. They would tell her that they couldn't do anything for at least twenty-four hours. She went back and forth, first thinking calling the police would be stupid, then thinking just the opposite. It didn't matter. More than likely what she had already done was stupid. Her life as she knew it might be just as over as it would have been if her husband had killed her. She finally decided that she would cover her back if she called the police. They wouldn't send anyone out, and she wouldn't call back. She might even call her mother to contact that detective, who might be able to help her out of her situation.

+++

"9-1-1. What is your emergency?"

"It's my husband."

"Do you mean your husband is in trouble, or your husband is causing trouble?"

"I guess he's in trouble. We're staying in a chalet outside of Gatlinburg and I went to the grocery and came back and he's not here."

"Maybe he went for a walk."

"My husband doesn't like the outdoors. I was even surprised when he suggested that we stay in a chalet in the mountains for a couple of weeks."

"Are you in the chalet now?"

"Yes."

"Is there any sign that there has been a struggle while you were gone?"

"No, everything looks pretty much the way it looked when I left."

"And you've searched everywhere? The bedroom? The bathroom? Out on the deck?"

"That's right. He's not in any of those places."

"Have you looked around outside to see if he might have stepped outdoors and fallen? Maybe he fell down a hill. I imagine there's a hill near where you are."

"Oh, yes. We have a big drop-off on the backside, away from the road."

"Maybe he fell there. Can you see over the railing without falling?"

"I don't know. I haven't checked."

"Well, I'll hold on while you check. Check around the outside, see if you see any trampled grass where he might have fallen."

"Okay, I'm taking the phone outside. I have a high-powered flashlight. I'm up on a walkway with a deck on the second level. I can see everything from here. I'm looking. I don't see anything. I think you need to send someone out."

"There's nothing we can do until he's been missing for twenty-four hours. Just call the regular number if he hasn't come back by then, or call 9-1-1 if you find him and he's injured."

"Okay. Thanks."

"Remember to call the regular police line if he hasn't returned or contacted you in twenty-four hours."

"I will."

Steve Demaree

14

Jack awoke, groggy, and unsure of where he was. He was leaning against something, but couldn't identify it. He tried to move, was able to move a little, but his restraints restricted his movement. Where was he? He wasn't sure. He looked around, although that ability, too, was limited. Some light penetrated from outside. He assumed it was the moon. But it wasn't enough for him to make out where he was. His head still felt funny, as if he had been drugged. He shook his head from side to side. Tried to think. Wherever he was he hadn't gotten there on his own. Someone had handcuffed him to something that felt like a pipe, and something else kept him from moving his feet.

A couple of minutes later Jack remembered he and Pam had been out somewhere. They were out driving. But he couldn't remember any more.

"Pam!" he hollered. The sound of his voice made his head hurt even more.

There was no answer. Whoever had done this had not bothered to gag him. That, and the fact that no one answered his call to his wife told him that wherever he was wasn't close enough for someone to hear him. Or if someone was nearby, they weren't coming to his aid.

Jack wondered where Pam was. Had someone abducted her? He remembered that she had been agitated about something. That was the reason he had suggested they go for a ride. Did they encounter someone on the ride? If so, what had they done with Pam?

+++

Even though it wasn't even 10:00 P.M., Pam went to bed. It took her a while to fall asleep.

The Fifth Day

Pam woke up the next morning, looked up at the shadows of the leaves dancing on the opposite wall, as the light came in from the glass windows high above her head. After a few seconds, she turned over to check on her husband, and then remembered what had happened the night before. Her body became rigid. She lay there, trying to relax.

Looking back on it she wished the detective had never called. She would rather have taken her chances with her husband, or someone he might have hired to murder her than to go through what she was going through at that moment. She wished she had someone to talk to. She got along okay with Carla, but she knew she couldn't talk to her. She wasn't close to Roz, Bernie's wife. And she couldn't talk to her mother about what she had done. Her mother would give her a biased opinion. She had a few friends back home that she might be able to talk to, but she didn't feel comfortable doing that at the moment. Besides, who's to say that any of her friends would have any better idea of what she should do than she would. And she wasn't close enough to any clergy to confide in them. For the time being at least, she was on her own. She alone had to determine her next step.

Steve Demaree

How does a woman whose husband is missing act?
Would she go out to look for him? Or would she remain
where she was, hoping he would soon show up, or some-
one would stop by with knowledge of his whereabouts?

Pam asked herself these questions as she lay there.
She had no idea how to answer them. She had never been
in this position before, but her best guess was that some
women would react one way, while other women would react another way.

+++

Jack awoke again, still tired. It was daylight. He
could tell he was in a rustic cabin. Light and a slight breeze
sneaked in through an occasional crack in the walls of the
wooden cabin. Jack was able to see a lot better than he did
when he woke the night before.

He assessed his situation. He was handcuffed to a
pipe that ran from the ceiling to a countertop that surrounded a sink that stood about waist high. He yanked on
the handcuff. It didn't come open. He took his free hand
and tried to pry it open. Another dead end. Then he took
that hand and felt for his pocketknife and his cell phone.
Whoever had done this to him and taken both of them.

He spotted several packages of crackers with peanut
butter lying on the counter in front of him. At least he
wouldn't go hungry. Well, at least not for a day or two. He
noticed the faucet, reached out with his free hand and
turned it. He had running water, too. It looked like all he
was missing was a bathroom and a soft recliner or bed
where he could rest.

Again he tried to move his feet. Something held them
in place. He was able to lean back just far enough to see
that someone had duct-taped them together and had secured them to something under the sink. He tried to reach
down, but he couldn't quite reach as far as his ankles.

His head somewhat clearer, he tried to figure out what to do. Whoever had done this to him had done a good job. It would take him hours to get free, provided he could ever get free.

He had a lot of money. Could it be that someone was holding him for ransom? Or could it be even worse? Could it be that Bernie planned to kill him and take control of the entire business? The way the agreement read if something happened to one partner the business reverted to the other partner. Oh, there would be plenty of money for Pam to live on, provided she was okay, but the business wouldn't be hers. It would all belong to Bernie. The thought of that caused him to struggle once again, trying to get free.

Jack listened. He thought he heard a car door shut. Was his attacker returning? Or could it be someone coming to rescue him? Or someone just happening by? Jack couldn't see outside to identify where he was. He didn't remember coming there the night before. Did someone knock him out somewhere else and bring him to the cabin? Because Jack had no idea where he was, he didn't know if there was a lot of traffic in the area. But he had heard a car door shut, so someone was nearby.

"I'm in here! Help!"

+++

For over an hour, Pam had thought about what she had done, and wondered what she should do next. She still had no idea. Should she go back and reason with Jack, flee the area, or stay where she was? In which one of these situations would she be safer? Was someone after her? Maybe someone Jack had hired? She looked over at the table a few feet away where she had laid Jack's gun. Did she even know how to fire it? She wasn't sure if she could fire that particular type of gun, but she could fire *a* gun. She wanted to check, but she didn't want a gunshot to bring someone running to the chalet, or the police. But she had taken some lessons in firing a gun after taking the self-defense class. And while she wasn't in the marksman class, she could probably hit a target lunging toward her, provided she noticed him in time.

With that in mind, Pam decided to stay at the cabin at least for one more day. In case someone stopped by, she would do her best to act as if nothing had happened. She knew that wasn't possible, but she would do what she could to pull it off. But then she figured that no one knew where they were staying, so she didn't expect any visitors. And the cops wouldn't stop by unless she called them again. And even they didn't know that she and Jack had rented a chalet. Or did they? Pam had no idea where Jack found out that the chalet was available. She never asked him. Maybe it belonged to a friend of his or one of his clients.

She thought of the police again. Should she call them? No, she didn't want to bring the police into it, at least not yet, and probably not at all, as long as she didn't spot anyone suspicious nearby. Should she go back to the cabin and check on Jack? No, she wouldn't do that. She'd left him enough food for him to survive for a few days. There were several packages of peanut butter and crackers. And she had heard that people can last for a few days without food. And Jack had running water, so he could sip enough with his good hand to keep him alive.

+++

Pam jumped when she heard the ringtone coming from Jack's phone. Beethoven's Fifth. But at that moment even *Gilligan's Island* would have caused her a fright. She wondered who it was, but didn't bother to answer it. She didn't even check to see if it was someone she knew. She had no answers for any inquisitive person at that moment. Whoever it was could think that Jack was away from his phone. If they knew he was on vacation, that would be a logical deduction for whoever was calling. And no one knew where they were, so even if they called back and suspected something they wouldn't come knocking at her door.

+++

Pam, tired of pacing back and forth from one side of the chalet to the other, took a short walk in the woods. That didn't help, so she returned to the chalet and tried to shoot pool, and then watch TV. That didn't work, either. But somehow Pam got through the day without throwing herself from the parapet of the top level of the chalet. But that was before she received a text, not long after dark.

WE KNOW WHAT YOU DID, AND WE KNOW WHERE YOU ARE. PLEASANT DREAMS!

Pam shook when she read the message. And the text was on her phone, not Jack's. Instead of a number, the phone read Private Caller. Who could it be? Who knew her number? Was it someone trying to scare her, or someone wanting her to lead them to Jack? She tried to reason but got nowhere. Her mother didn't know how to send a text. She had taken Jack's phone, so it wasn't him, or someone who had kidnapped him using his phone. Could it have been Bernie, who was trying to find out where Jack was? Or whoever that was who called from the Berium Corporation? They had called her phone, not Jack's. So, they had her number, too. And she and Jack had left town the day after they called. Maybe they had stopped by the office, and the house, and were unable to locate Jack. And their only other way to get in touch with him was to call her. Pam's thoughts moved from who called to where had they called from, as in location. Could they be outside, or just down the road?

She grabbed the gun and headed for the front door. She moved slowly, even though she knew there was no one else inside the chalet. She approached the door, stood next to it and listened. She heard nothing, no one. She held the gun in her right hand, ready to fire. She took her left hand and opened the door. Slightly at first, and then all the way when no one came rushing inside. Instead of walking outside she picked up a shoe and tossed it out onto the walkway. No one rushed the doorway when she did it, so she stepped outside. She went back inside the house and picked up a Maglite LED flashlight, a powerful one that the owners had left for them to use. She flicked the switch. The batteries were good, so she headed back to the door, clumsily opened it, while trying to hold on to the gun and the flashlight. She stepped out onto the walkway, shined the light from one side of the property to the other, saw no one. She walked up to her car, turning around almost every other step to make sure no one slipped into the house while she was out of it. She bent over, shined the light underneath her car. There was nothing. Not even an oil leak left by a previous tenant. She stepped back away from the vehicle, and walked around it, still shining the light. There was no one there. The flashlight had a high-powered beam, so she shined it in each direction, up and down the road, but there were no movements, no cars anywhere. As far as she could tell, she was alone. As she retreated to the chalet, she heard a noise, saw movement from out of the corner of her eye. But it was only a squirrel that Pam had disturbed with her nocturnal venture.

She walked back in, surveyed the house to make sure she was alone. There was no one else. Pam felt slightly safer inside, knowing that the house was locked up tight, and knowing that a bullet moves faster than an intruder. But there were no intruders. Pam wondered if the message was intended for her. She assumed that it was, but sometimes people get the wrong number. And then she wondered if whoever it was knew what she had done to Jack and if they did know where she was. She doubted it, but she felt certain that unless it had been a wrong number that whoever it was had done it to frighten her. On that note, they were successful.

15

The Sixth Day

Pam awoke the next morning in no better mental state than she was in the day before. Or for that matter, at any time after she received a call from the detective her mother hired. Could he have been the one who called on Jack's phone a few times the day before? No. He would have called her on her phone, and her phone rang only once. That call had been from her mother, and she was in no state of mind to talk to her mother. She hoped her mother didn't worry when she couldn't get hold of her. And then she remembered the text. Who could that have been? A good night's sleep hadn't taken away her fear.

Not long after breakfast, Pam's state of mind was about to get worse. As she carried her dishes to the sink someone knocked on the door. It was all she could do to keep from dropping her plate and glass.

She wondered who it was and reached for the gun. Surely it wasn't the person her husband had hired to kill her. They wouldn't knock first. Or would they? Would they try to gain her confidence?

She walked slowly to the door. Whoever it was knocked again. So did Pam's knees. The deadbolt was on, but the place had enough windows that if someone wanted to harm her badly enough they could throw something through a window and come charging in. And the bullets from her gun could go charging out. She felt somewhat safe, as long as there was only one intruder.

"Who is it?"

"It's the police. I have a couple of questions for you?"

"How do I know you're the police?"

"You can tell if you open the door. Are you Mrs. Archer? A Mrs. Archer called 9-1-1 the night before last."

Pam opened the door but left the latch chain on. On the other side of the door stood a tall man in a policeman's uniform. He seemed to be the outdoor type, and she judged him to be in his early forties. He flashed her a wallet, that when opened contained a badge and an ID card.

"Just a minute while I take the chain off."

The policeman nodded, and Pam closed the door and released the chain.

"Please come in."

The policeman looked at her.

"I will as long as you promise not to shoot me."

Pam looked at him, and he motioned with his head toward the gun she still clutched much too tightly.

"Oh, I'm sorry. But it's better to be safe than sorry."

"It is, but I'll feel safer if you'll put that gun down."

"Oh, uh, sure. So, how did you find me? I don't remember giving my name and address the other night."

"We are the police, Mrs. Archer. We have our ways. And by the way, I'm Sgt. Cletus Culpepper of the Sevier County Police Department. Here's my card."

Pam took his card, put it down on the table.

"Good to meet you, Sgt. Culpepper. And I guess you do have ways of finding folks. So, what brings you way up here today?"

"Well, you did call and say your husband was missing. Is he back by any chance?"

"No. I'm sorry. I'm not thinking too clearly right now. You haven't found him?"

"No, would you happen to have a picture of him?"

"Just at home."

"That's okay. We can come up with one. That is, I assume you still want us to look for him."

"Uh, yeah, sure. I hope he hasn't wandered off somewhere and fallen and hurt himself."

"According to the call you placed the other night, he isn't likely to do that."

"No, he isn't."

"Could he have gone back home and not let you know?"

"Not unless someone picked him up. I still have the SUV, the one out front. And Jack would never go home without telling me, anyway."

"And you have no idea where he might be?"

Pam paused, maybe a little too long.

"I was trying to think. We've never been to this area before, and as far as I know, Jack doesn't know anyone down this way."

"Well, Mrs. Archer, is there anything else I can do for you? If not, we'll get to work looking for your husband."

"No, you go right ahead."

"Oh, I almost forgot. I found this envelope lying beside the door. It has your name on it. Seems like someone tried to raise you and wasn't successful."

"For me? You must be mistaken. No one knows I'm here."

"Well, it has your name on it. Would you like me to open it and read it?"

"No. No. That's okay."

"Well, do you want me to wait while you read it?"

"No. I can do it later. In a few minutes."

"What if it's a ransom note? Your husband does have a lot of money, doesn't he?"

"How did you know that?"

"We did a short check on him to see if it would help us find him if he's still missing."

"Well, you're right. He does have a lot of money. But no one knew we were coming down here. We didn't even tell his business partner."

"So how would anyone be able to get in touch with him, provided there was an emergency?"

"Well, we both have cell phones."

"Have you tried calling his cell phone?"

"Uh, it wouldn't do any good."

"Bad reception?"

"In some places. But his cell phone is here."

"So, he left in a hurry."

"Evidently. Listen, Sgt. Culpepper, this whole ordeal has me worn to a frazzle. Would it be okay if we talked about this another time?"

"Okay. As you wish. We'll keep looking for him. Anyway, you have my card. Feel free to call me if you need anything. And call me personally. I'll be the most up to date of any of the officers because I'm the officer in charge of this case."

"Okay. I'll do that if I need you."

"Well, Good day, and don't worry. We have everything under control."

+++

When Sgt. Culpepper handed Pam that envelope immediately she put her hands behind her so that he couldn't see them shaking. When he left, she waited until she saw his cruiser drive away before she looked at the envelope for the first time. It had her name on it, in large block letters. Who could it be? Had someone seen her put Jack in that cabin, and if so, were they blackmailing her?

She rushed to open the envelope, which made it harder to open. She gave up and located a knife to slit it open. Mission accomplished, she put the knife down, blew on the envelope, and reached in to retrieve the paper inside. It was a tight fit. It took her a few seconds to remove the paper and unfold it. Then she read it and gasped.

WE HAVE YOUR HUSBAND. DON'T CALL THE POLICE. DOING SO WILL CAUSE US TO SEND YOUR HUSBAND BACK TO YOU ONE BODY PART AT A TIME. BE AT PANCAKE PANTRY TOMORROW MORNING AT 10:00. IF YOU ARE NOT THERE, YOU WILL FIND YOUR HUSBAND'S WEDDING RING AND RING FINGER OUTSIDE YOUR CABIN DOOR.

Pam collapsed onto the couch. Did someone have Jack? Had he been kidnapped? She was sure that no one had followed them. She saw no other cars, no one on foot. Was this a joke? Was it merely a coincidence that she had hid Jack somewhere a couple of days before someone sent the note. Or could it be that someone was watching her and noticed that Jack was no longer with her? That would make more sense.

She contemplated what to do. She wanted to call the police, or at least the private detective her mother had

Should she drive back to the ramshackle cabin to see if Jack was there? Was this all a ploy by someone who wanted to locate Jack, someone who was waiting for her to lead them to him? Or was someone trying to lure her out into the open for some reason or another? Should she go for a drive, headed nowhere in particular, to see if someone followed her? And was the person who delivered the note the same person who sent her the text the night before. The night before. She pictured it in her mind. She wasn't sure where the policeman said he found the envelope, but regardless, even in the dark, Pam was sure there wasn't an envelope near the door the night before. Whoever left it had visited her that morning, without her hearing him.

She contemplated what to do. She wanted to call the police, or at least the private detective her mother had hired, but she was afraid that whoever was responsible for the note would find out and something bad would happen to Jack.

Pam tried to calm down so she could think clearly and rationally. She tried to block everything out of her mind, except what she should do next. After she wasn't shaking as much and breathing as heavily, she assessed her situation. She would do as the person had said. She wouldn't contact anyone, and she would go to Pancake Pantry the next morning. She would leave in time so that if she had to wait in line, she would be seated inside the restaurant at 10:00. Besides, she didn't think anyone would try something there. She would have been more alarmed if he had recommended the most remote scenic overlook. But then maybe someone had suggested the Pancake Pantry merely as a starting point, and that someone planned to follow Pam when she left. But that thought never entered her mind.

16

The Seventh Day

Pam left the chalet early, just in case traffic was heavy. It wasn't until she arrived in Gatlinburg. Not wanting to waste a lot of time looking for a place to park, once again she opted for the first parking lot she could find. She looked down the street, saw no trolleys moving in the direction she was to head, so after she paid for her parking she took off on foot. Pam walked up the hill toward Pancake Pantry. Well, it wasn't as if the popular restaurant was on a hill, but there was an incline, one that you wouldn't notice if you were driving, but would if you were on foot. She looked around. The closer she got to the center of town, the heavier the traffic was. Cars were moving slowly in both directions. She wasn't sure if that was a good thing or a bad thing. It would be harder for her to spot someone, but it would also be harder for someone to do her harm. She passed River Road, looked over and saw the Aquarium. She had only another block and a half to go if she remembered correctly. She checked her phone to see the time. 9:23. She was in plenty of time. She wasn't told to get there at 10:00, but to be there at 10:00. Maybe she would get there early, eat, and be there before her adversary entered the restaurant.

A Smoky Mountain Mystery

As she neared the restaurant she saw the line for the first time. Everyone else must have received a note, too, or a lot of people had been responsible for her receiving the note and had come to meet her. She tried to smile at her attempt at humor, hoping it would help her during her trying time. Seeing the growing line, she quickened her pace, knowing that finding a place in line thirty seconds early might save her five minutes or more of waiting to enter the restaurant. Pam checked those already in line as she passed them and headed to the end of the line. None of them looked familiar. She assumed that whoever came to meet her would be one person by himself. At least she assumed it was a man. What if there were two of them? One person by himself would be easier to spot. Well, maybe not. Maybe two suspicious men would be easier. So, it must be two people, a man, and a woman. Or a man and a woman with children. Immediately she thought of the crude drawings on the back of some minivans, the ones that told how many men, women, children, dogs, and cats were part of that particular family. She shook her head to get her mind back to the business at hand.

Pam arrived at the end of the line. There were around twenty people in front of her. Before turning to take her place she looked at the paved path beside the restaurant that led back to a multitude of shops in a picturesque setting. She had heard that many of the shops sold items vacationers were still glad they had purchased after they arrived back home. The shops didn't merely sell knickknacks, but expensive works of art, as well. If circumstances had been different, Pam would have eaten a leisurely breakfast, possibly sat on a bench by the street and watched all the passersby for a few minutes, before being enticed by those quaint little shops and what they sold. But this was not one of those days.

The harried woman looked up and down the street. There were lots of people. On both sides of the street. She figured if one of them was whoever was looking for her, that person would be stationary. That would make him easier to spot because most of the people were on their way to their destination, most of them someplace other than Pancake Pantry. She looked for a head that resembled a periscope, rotating, checking out the crowd. Or if her antagonist was nervous, he might look like someone watching a tennis match from center court. Although a stereotypical villain might be hiding behind a newspaper, or standing, or sitting casually on a bench on the other side of the street. Or maybe whoever it was, was already seated inside the restaurant, waiting for her. Or maybe standing out of the way, waiting for her. Would he attempt to join her as soon as she was seated, accost her as she left, or slip her another note trying to lure her to a more secluded spot.

She had brought the gun. She wasn't sure if that was a good idea or a bad one, but she decided to err on the side of caution. But she didn't plan to lay it on the table while she ate. There was no need to cause pandemonium unless she needed to do so to get away safely.

A slight breeze blew her hair as she stood, looking around casually, doing her best to fit in and look like a tourist. Well, she was on a vacation, and before the phone call and the fiasco with her husband she looked and acted the part, even though she was a rookie. Pam looked up, above the shops on the other side of the street up into the mountains. There was an occasional house. One of them looked quite large. Probably had a gate and bodyguards. That would be a likely place for someone to hold her husband hostage. She didn't see anyone standing in front of that house, holding an enormous ransom note. But she didn't think they would hold a rich man in a ramshackle cabin. Well, not unless she was the one who did it, but she only did so because she didn't have much time to think beforehand.

A Smoky Mountain Mystery

When she left the restaurant, if she was still clueless as to where to find her husband, she wondered if she should she drive through the mountains looking for him. She quickly arrived at an intelligent conclusion. No, that would be stupid, a waste of time.

The man behind her tapped her on the shoulder. Like most unsuspecting people would do, she jumped. Was this it? Her contact? She slipped her hand down into her large purse and gripped the gun as she turned to confront him. He merely pointed, and she turned to realize that while she was daydreaming of being Wonder Woman, or the frightened protagonist in an Alfred Hitchcock movie, the line had moved on. She was almost to the door.

Five minutes later she was seated at a table near the front window, where she could see anyone who walked up the street toward the restaurant. Her server, a middle-aged woman, had greeted her and gone off to fill her drink order. Pam wasn't surprised to find her server was middle-aged, as opposed to the college students she was used to at home. She had heard that people who worked at Pancake Pantry stayed for years.

Pam glanced at the menu the server had handed her. She wasn't exactly of a mind to peruse the menu and savor each delicacy. Instead, she pointed at one item and ordered it when her server returned with some coffee, and two glasses, one containing water with lemon, the other orange juice.

Pam drummed her fingers on the table while she waited for her food. Each time she caught herself doing this she stopped. Each time she thought of her predicament, she started drumming again.

She looked up, anxious for her server to bring her food. She didn't know why. She wasn't all that hungry. But the food would occupy her mind. She took out her phone and checked the time. 10:03. Okay, he was here somewhere. But where? She tried to be casual as she skirted the restaurant with her eyes, looking for a familiar face. And then she saw him and clutched the table with both hands. It was one of the two strangers she had seen when she had eaten there before. The man looked at his watch, then looked at her and smiled. Would he wait until she left before he approached her?

Pam almost jumped when her server arrived with her food.

"I didn't mean to scare you."

"Oh, that's okay. I had my mind on something else and I didn't see you."

"Is everything okay?"

"Uh, sure. Why do you ask?"

"Oh, I don't know. You just look like something's bothering you. I didn't mean to meddle."

"No, I'm fine."

The woman sat the food down, asked if Pam needed anything else, and then left after Pam had told her "no."

I guess they wouldn't expect me to suspect it was a woman, an older woman, a server at that. Could she be the one who has me unnerved? No, it has to be the strange man.

Pam wasn't sure how quickly to eat. She turned and looked at the stranger. His food had arrived, too. He was eating, but he didn't seem to be in a hurry. She followed his lead, ate casually as if nothing was on her mind. She looked out the window, even smiled and waved to a little girl, who smiled and waved to her. She shook her head when her thoughts turned to *they wouldn't expect me to suspect a little girl, a cute one who smiled. Maybe someone promised that little girl an ice cream cone if she did as they said.*

Twenty minutes later, Pam was proud of herself. She managed to eat her breakfast, actually enjoy it, without spilling anything or knocking anything off the table.

Her server had checked with her again to see if she wanted more coffee, which Pam declined, then checked a final time as she was finishing her meal.

"You're a popular lady."

"Excuse me?"

"First a woman handed me a note, asked me to give it to you when I brought you your check. Then a man handed me a second note, asked me if I would give it to you. Kind of reminded me of spy stuff. At least I'll tell it like that when I get home tonight. My husband always asks me how my day went. Anyway, here's your check, and here are the two notes."

"Are you sure they're for me?"

"Yes, both people pointed to you. I wanted to make sure I gave them to the right person. I wouldn't want to give them to the wrong person if they are personal."

The server thanked Pam for coming in, then turned away. She would read the notes, then, if no one approached her, pay the cashier and leave.

Pam looked at the two notes. One wasn't even in an envelope. The other was in an envelope like the one the policeman had handed her. She turned and looked for the stranger, but he was gone. Was he the man who sent her one of the notes?

Pam wiped off the table knife with her napkin and sliced open the envelope. Once again paper was jammed inside an envelope. She yanked it out, opened it, and began to read.

CROSS THE STREET. WALK TOWARD LIGHT 8. YOU WILL SEE A SKYLIFT. TAKE IT TO THE TOP. WE WILL TALK THERE.

It sounded like something out of a World War II spy movie. Was someone planning to push her over the edge of the mountain? She had come this far. She planned to follow through. Besides, the gun gave her more confidence. But she wouldn't get too close to the edge of the cliff.

Pam almost forgot about the second note, until she noticed it on the table. She picked it up and opened it.

Meet me in the women's restroom as soon as you read this.

Could it be that some woman had some information for her? Maybe this woman had seen the man watching Pam and wanted to warn her. But why wouldn't she approach Pam at her table? The man was gone. But then she might have been afraid that he was still watching, which would have put her in a precarious position.

Pam paid for her food at the register and grasped the stairway railing with her left hand. She climbed the steps on the wrong side as she mounted them to the women's restroom. She was almost to the landing when she heard two pairs of small feet plop down on the landing a foot or so in front of her. Quickly she moved over, dodged a boy and a girl, both trying to be the first one to the bottom. Next came a woman frantically trying to keep up with the two youngsters as they headed down the stairs.

"Sorry,," the woman said, as she hurried after her charges.

The woman was gone before Pam could mumble something or smile at the woman.

Pam made it to the top, looked ahead and saw a railing, a railing that allowed someone the opportunity to stand there and look down at all the people dining on the level below. Could it be that someone had observed her from this vantage point? If so, that left out the man she had seen. Except for the last time, he had been at his table the whole time. At least she thought so. Did that mean he wasn't one of the kidnappers? Again Pam wished for someone by her side, someone she could trust.

17

Pam wanted to rush over, look down into the restaurant, and see if she saw someone suspicious, but then she remembered a woman was waiting for her in the restroom. Well, supposedly there was a woman. She hoped someone hadn't lured her up there to kidnap her. Once again she shoved her hand down into her purse until she located the gun. She had been careful to leave the safety on.

Pam turned left toward the restrooms, and as she saw the woman standing ten or so feet in front of her, her mouth flew open.

"Were you the one who sent this note?"

"Well, I didn't want to cause a scene in a busy restaurant. So, where's Jack?"

"What do you mean, 'Where's Jack?'"

"Well, he is your husband, isn't he? And the two of you did come down here on vacation. And here you are eating alone. So, where's Jack?"

"Carla, you know Jack. He's not big in going out in a large group of people."

"He's not big on answering his cell phone, either. I've been trying to get hold of him, and he hasn't answered since the other night when he had to go quickly because you'd been out and had just returned."

"How did you find me? Did Jack tell you where we were?"

"I asked, but he didn't tell me."

"Have you got something going on with my husband?"

"What? Of course not. What we were talking about is work-related. It's a time-sensitive matter. That's the reason I came down here when I couldn't reach him after I had tried many times over a several hour period."

"And how did you know I was going to be eating here today? Were you the one who sent the note?"

"Of course, I sent the note. Do you see anyone else up here? Maybe you should check the restroom. Maybe another woman is waiting for you."

"I meant the other note."

"What other note?"

"Never mind. You still haven't told me how you knew that Jack and I were in Gatlinburg."

"I overheard Bernie talking to someone, said Jack took off for the Smokies."

"Jack told me he didn't tell Bernie where he was going."

"I don't know about that. I just know that Bernie knows Jack is down here somewhere."

"And how did you know that I was going to be at Pancake Pantry this morning?"

"I didn't. I got down here yesterday. With Gatlinburg being more compact that Pigeon Forge I figured my best chance of finding the two of you would be here. I wandered the streets yesterday, looking at everyone who passed by. Then I'm out again this morning and I see you striding up the street like you're in a hurry to get to someone or away from someone. So, I watched to see if you were meeting someone. When no one joined you by the time you got through eating, I scribbled a note and handed it to your server, asked her if she would give it to you when you got ready to pay your bill. Then I came up here to wait for you. So, what is this about another note?"

"Never mind."

"So, where's Jack?"

"He wanted to be alone for a while, so I came into town."

"So, you're staying in some cabin somewhere. That doesn't sound like Jack."

"No, it doesn't, but Jack was the one who rented it. I just told him that he needed to take a vacation. Jack picked the place. It surprised me, too. And it's more than a cabin. It's a chalet, pretty good size, but I've seen larger since we got here."

"I still think you're not telling me everything."

"And I think you're hiding something, too."

"So, where are you headed next?"

"To see a few sights. Alone."

"That means I'm not invited?"

"You're smarter than I thought."

"What's with the snippy attitude?"

"It's just that I didn't expect to see you. If Jack and I had wanted to be bothered while we're here, we would have announced to the world where we were going."

"And you're not going to tell me where I can find Jack?"

"He's tied up. He said he didn't want to be disturbed for a while, told me to go into town and have fun for a few hours while he finished what he was doing."

"And I don't assume you know what that was."

"I have no interest in Jack's business."

"And you won't tell me anything else?"

Pam didn't know how to answer, but she wasn't about to let Carla know her predicament. Carla wasn't her main problem, but she was anxious to get rid of her so she could meet whoever sent her the other note, the one that resembled the first note she received, the one handed to her by the Tennessee policeman.

+++

Pam was anxious to get to the top of the mountain, but she waited until Carla got tired of getting no additional answers, and left. After Carla walked down the stairs, Pam walked over to the railing, looked down into the restaurant, but didn't recognize anyone. And no one felt her eyes upon them and cast theirs up at her. She didn't even see anyone hiding behind a newspaper or a large pair of sunglasses.

She was tired of wasting time. She needed to find the sky lift. Unlike her eagerness to get to the top of the stairs to see who had left a note for her, she descended slowly, back to the first floor of the restaurant, with no one bounding up the steps to accost her, and no children in her path. She looked in every direction for a familiar face or someone who looked interested in her. As she left the restaurant, there was no line to get inside. Most of the breakfast crowd had eaten. Most of the lunch crowd hadn't arrived.

Pam scanned the street. Still no recognizable faces. Not even Carla. But she hadn't noticed Carla as she was on her way to the restaurant, either. Pam's trek was still uphill. She was told to cross the street, so she did so, as soon as there was a lull in the traffic.

Five minutes later she had found the sky lift. The front side was merely a small building right off the sidewalk next to the street. She walked around, looked at the other side. Nothing but cables, and bench-like seats transporting people to the top of the mountain, as if they were going skiing. Again, no one looked familiar or interested in her.

She walked back to the front, looked up and down the street, and scanned the area. No one seemed interested in her. Not wanting to waste any more time, she stepped up to the window, bought a ticket, and listened to the ticket seller's instructions to follow the serpentine railing to the back. There was nothing special about the railing. It looked like so many others she had seen keeping people in line for amusement park rides. There were a few people in front of her, mostly couples, or adults with children.

When it came her time, Pam felt the bench seat hit her on her upper thighs. She sat down the way the operator had instructed her to do, and a bar lowered to keep her in place. Pam moved slowly upward, out over top River Road, twenty or thirty feet or so off the ground. She was a sitting target, but no one seemed interested in her. She looked one way, then the other, as she passed over the road. It was late enough in the morning that enough people had already arrived and free parking spaces on River Road were few and far between, and mostly on the edge of town.

The lift moved up the mountain. There were trees to the left of her, more trees to her right. The trees had been removed from the area below her to allow the sky lift to function. Pam was surprised to find that she wasn't as high off the ground as she expected to be. Maybe it was just enough distance to kill her if she fell, but the bar locking her in place prevented that from happening.

She looked over to the left to the people who had already been to the top of the mountain and were on their way back down. Some were couples. Some were older children. Some appeared to be college students, wearing shirts with their college's name on them. Some were talking to their seatmate. Others were taking in the beautiful scenery. None of them had a ransom note or a gun aimed at her. None of them looked familiar. All of them looked happier than she was. Most looked like they didn't have a care in the world. Vacations are like that, as long as your spouse doesn't get kidnapped, or isn't suspected of wanting to murder you. Pam wondered how different things would have been if she hadn't left Jack in that abandoned cabin. Would she still have been alive?

Pam was in the moment. She turned and looked behind, the best she could. There was no sign of the man she'd seen twice at Pancake Pantry, the other man she saw there that would scare her if she saw him in a dark alley, and she didn't see Carla. Maybe all three of them were at the top, waiting on her.

As Pam neared the top, a camera snapped her picture. A sign a few feet lower on the mountain had warned her to be ready for it. Pam realized that this was another attraction looking to take advantage of any situation to make money any way they could. Well, she wouldn't be buying a photo of herself.

Pam's feet hit the ground, and she stepped from the sky lift. An older man seated in a chair gave her something she could hand to someone inside the building who would show her the photo. Her first couple of steps were awkward. She looked around. It wasn't a large area. It would be hard not to be seen. Maybe whoever had sent her the note had arrived before her, seen that the place wasn't as isolated as they thought, and left before she arrived. The man she suspected as being the one who sent the note did leave the restaurant several minutes before she did, even before she was delayed by Carla. But then again, maybe he was here. Or maybe whoever sent her the note had noticed that she had been delayed at the restaurant. Maybe he or she hadn't arrived yet. She didn't see anyone familiar, but she would wait, even though she lacked the patience to do so.

She walked over and stood at the edge of the mountain, looked down at the ants crawling along well down below her, and at the Matchbox cars that trickled down River Road and the Parkway. If the person who had written the note to her was down there, she was certain that he couldn't see her and she couldn't see him.

"It's a long way down, isn't it?"

She turned to face a woman who was fifty years her senior.

"Yes, it is. But if we start with a good roll it shouldn't take long to get to the bottom."

"Now that I'm getting older, I prefer the slower method of descending."

"I hope to get older, so I prefer the same method. Slow and easy wins the race."

The woman excused herself when her cell phone rang. Seconds later Pam received a text. Like the other one, this text was from an unknown caller.

ENJOYING THE VIEW? I HEARD THAT SOME-TIMES THOSE BARS THAT LOCK YOU IN PLACE COME LOOSE, AND IT'S WORSE TO FALL OUT ON THE WAY DOWN.

As Pam finished reading the text, she turned quickly, hoping to find a guilty-looking person. Was whoever sent the message close enough to have heard her talking to the older woman? As best she remembered, there was no one standing nearby at the time. She looked at the older woman, standing not more than fifteen feet from her, still on her cell phone, and not looking the least bit guilty.

When Pam left home, she didn't know she was going to ride a sky lift to the top of a mountain, but someone might have known. Either that someone was on top of the mountain with her, was below but had seen her go up, or had left her the note and was guessing that she was atop the mountain at that moment. She didn't think the last choice was all that good, but she didn't think whoever texted her was near her. Regardless, whoever sent her the note and the text, whether they were the same person or not, was either someone she knew who was doing a good job of hiding from her, or someone she didn't know who was doing a good job of not looking suspicious.

Pam didn't want the person to know that the text un-nerved her, so she decided to remain at the top for a few more minutes. She looked around some more, mainly checking out those who arrived after she did. Each bench seat arrived with one or two new people. None of them looked familiar. None of them looked like kidnappers. Well, a few did, but they were from other countries. She wondered if whoever had written the note was European or a Middle Easterner. There was nothing in the note that showed that.

As Pam stood there, she got an idea. If the camera had taken her picture, it had also taken a photo of everyone else who had ventured up the mountain that day. Even those who had arrived and left before she did, who left without purchasing their photo. Pam eased over to the small building where the young man stood, hawking the photos. She looked at the photographed faces she saw smiling from a bench seat but saw no one she recognized. There was no one holding a card with her name on it. But that would be true until her husband's kidnapper was a limo driver at the airport.

"Here's your photo."

"I'm not interested. Maybe if I come back and my husband comes up with me the second time, but he's a little afraid of heights, so I doubt if he will do it. I was checking to see if a friend of mine had been up here. I don't think he would have purchased his photo, either."

"Well, here's the ones we have. We keep all of them for an hour before discarding them."

Pam looked over the pictures, recognized no one except the older lady who spoke to her. She had come up with a young person, probably her granddaughter. From the photo, the girl looked like she might be in high school or college.

As Pam stepped away, she changed her mind. If the man had come up on the sky lift, he might have purchased his photo, so no one else would see it.

Several more minutes passed, and no one had approached her. She wondered how long she was to remain where she was. Was someone keeping her waiting to make her more nervous?

She noticed some machines by the overlook, machines that would allow her to magnify those ants below so that they looked like dogs, cats, or small humans. People were looking through some of them, but a couple of them were free so Pam walked over to one of them, deposited her money, and put her eye to the magnifier. The magnification wasn't enough to allow her to identify someone in case there was a lineup later, but she looked at buildings. She familiarized herself with the structures she could see on the far side of the Parkway, then looked up at the trees and other objects on the mountain on the other side of Gatlinburg. She noticed a couple of hotels but doubted if anyone was holding her husband in one of them. Thirty minutes later she ended her wild-goose chase, and once again a seat bumped against her upper thighs. Unless someone accosted her on her way back to her SUV, it was time to go back to the chalet. Maybe the next day she would return to the ramshackle cabin where she had left her husband to see if all of this was a hoax. Could it be that her husband had escaped and was getting even with her?

18

Pam checked the bar that held her in place to make sure it was secure. As the sky lift started down and Pam's eyes dropped to the town well below, she thought back to the text she had received. There was nothing in the text that helped Pam identify the person who sent it. And she knew that whoever it was could only use so many characters and blank spaces. All she could tell was that whoever sent it wasn't illiterate. Psychotic maybe, but not illiterate.

A few minutes later, her ride had reached the bottom, back down in the hustle and bustle of Gatlinburg, where Pam had gotten on to ride up to the top of the mountain. As she got off, she studied the people she saw. None of them were familiar. None of them looked threatening. So, she reverted to her persona as a person on vacation, with not a care in the world. She walked up the right-hand side of the street, checking out small shops, and people who might look like kidnappers. She looked across the street and saw the Convention Center. She wondered what went on in there. Before she knew it, she had arrived at Light 10, crossed the street, and started walking down the far side, toward Pancake Pantry, and beyond, to her car. She had gone a few blocks before a child's squeal and a familiar smell wafted through the air to where she stood. She found herself back at Fanny Farkel's. She stood there, taking in her surroundings.

A Smoky Mountain Mystery

After a few seconds, she realized that she was standing in the middle of the sidewalk, and people were having to go around her. If they hadn't been on vacation and in a happy mood, they might have given her a dirty look or an unkind word as they passed. Her stomach growled, and she checked the time on her phone and found out it was lunchtime. She walked up to the man behind the counter and ordered. A few minutes later, she stepped away to an unoccupied bench and sat down with her sausage and drink. She took a bite, and for a minute she forgot that she wasn't in heaven. She sat there and devoured the sausage, relishing every bite. While she ate she saw a boy, who looked like he was somewhere between eight and ten years old. He stepped up to the counter and order an Ogle dog, while his sister cashed in her arcade tickets for a stuffed animal. Pam hadn't had an Ogle dog, but to hear people tell it, it was a longer and better-tasting version of what Pam knew as a corn dog. Pam could tell both the boy and the girl were having fun, as were their parents, who stood about ten feet away keeping their eyes on both charges.

Pam remained there for a few minutes after she finished eating, trying to act like she was enjoying her vacation, and trying not to look like a woman who didn't know where to turn. After she sat there a few minutes and digested her lunch, Pam did a very un-Pam-like thing. She walked into the arcade. She hadn't played Skee-Ball since she was a teenager, but she stopped and played a few games. Between games, she turned to check and see if anyone had followed her inside. No one had. After she had had her fill of Skee-Ball, she spotted a couple of games from days gone by, Pac-Man and Centipede. She played both, as well as Wheel of Fortune, collected the tickets she had won, and handed them to a little girl who was playing games, trying to win a stuffed animal. As Pam handed the tickets to the little girl's mother, the child squealed with delight.

Pam felt she had spent enough time in Gatlinburg, enough time pretending to be a tourist who wasn't afraid of anything. She walked several blocks until she returned to her car. She could have taken a trolley. She saw trolleys with different color names, each headed to a different destination, but she couldn't remember what color she wanted. And it was too much for Pam to study the map to see which trolley stopped closest to where she had parked. She was physically and emotionally drained when she fell into the driver's seat of her car. She got in, locked her vehicle, and continued to be cautious, looking this way and that. The parking lot was full of cars, but she seemed to be the only human there. She wasn't sure if that was good or bad.

She had no interest in doing any more sightseeing, so she drove down the hill and turned right onto the East Parkway. Thirty minutes or so later, she returned to her chalet. She got out of her vehicle and spun around slowly to see if she had company. There appeared to be no one, but someone had been there.

A few steps short of the front door she looked up and spotted another envelope. It matched the two previous envelopes. She punched her code to enter, grabbed the latest note, and rushed into her vacation home that didn't seem much like one. She tore the paper from the envelope, opened it and read.

I'M GLAD YOU KEPT YOUR APPOINTMENT. FOR THE TIME BEING YOUR HUSBAND WILL KEEP ALL HIS FINGERS. BUT THERE SEEMS TO BE SOMEONE ELSE INTERESTED IN YOU, TOO, WHICH PREVENTED ME FROM MAKING CONTACT, BUT WE WILL TRY AGAIN TOMORROW. SAME TIME, SAME PLACE. AND JUST IN CASE I SEE ANOTHER INTERESTED PARTY TOMOR-ROW AND CAN'T JOIN YOU FOR BREAKFAST, STICK AROUND TOWN, BROWSE THROUGH THE SHOPS

NEARBY. IF WE HAVEN'T MET BY THEN, CHECK OUT
HILLBILLY GOLF AT TRAFFIC LIGHT 2, AND BE SURE
NOT TO OVERHIT YOUR PUTTS.

Pam reread the note and thought back to the text.
From what she could ascertain, the same person wrote
both of them. But who was that person? Could it be that
the person saw her at Pancake Pantry and drove away immediately to her chalet, to leave her another note? But then
how would he have known she was up on the mountain?
Maybe there were two of them. But how could it be two
people and the writing be similar in style? And then she
thought there could be two if they split up. They could have
stayed in touch by phone, and the person who wasn't ob-
serving Pam could have let the other one know where she
was. She was having a hard time thinking one person
would do this, but two sounded more plausible. But what
if it was only one person? Had he been at Pancake Pantry,
or up on the mountain? Or was he somewhere in town,
watching her from a distance? If so, she didn't see him, unless he was the stranger she had seen twice at Pancake Pantry. Or was the stranger at the restaurant the one who prevented her from making contact with the kidnapper? Or
could it be that he was talking about Carla? Had he seen
her?

Pam studied the note some more. Whoever wrote it
wasn't illiterate, although maybe he had tried to look that
way with the block letters he used. No, this wasn't someone
who planned to use the ransom money to pull himself up
out of poverty. But so far there was no mention of money.
What did this guy want? Why had he kidnapped her husband, provided he did kidnap him?

If Pam wasn't tired before, she certainly was by this
time. Her arms and legs ached. Her back ached. Even her
head ached. She hurried to the door, looked out quickly,

and saw no one. Whoever it was had left. Or so she thought.

Pam walked out on to the deck, saw the hot tub, walked over, removed the cover, and turned the knob to get the water ready for her. There was no other cabin, or any human being in sight. She gave the hot tub a few minutes to warm up, then took off her clothes and stepped into the warm water and sat down. No one could get to her except through the house, and her gun was within an arm's reach if someone burst through the front door. Even where she was she could have it aimed at someone's heart before they could get within ten feet of her. And if there was more than one they would have to come at her from the same direction. She could mow them down in order. She felt safe, at least in the cabin, during the day.

A few minutes in the hot tub helped. Pam stepped out and picked up a towel to dry herself. She stood there and looked out over God's beautiful mountainside, then walked inside to contemplate what she planned to do.

19

The Eighth Day

Pam awoke the next morning and picked up her phone to check the time. 7:32. Plenty of time to take a shower and head to town to see if the kidnapper shows up. If he didn't meet her at the restaurant, Pam had already decided she would do as he said. Act as a single woman on a vacation to Gatlinburg would do, as she did before, and check out more of what the small town surrounded by mountains had to offer. She couldn't believe that a town where only 4,000 people live could offer so much and attract so many to the area. She wondered what the people of Gatlinburg thought of so many tourists, and how much they look forward to the offseason, which she assumed was winter. But then don't mountains attract skiers? Or are there too many trees on these mountains?

Not wanting to adapt to a pattern where the kidnapper would know her every move, she arrived before 9:00 and lucked out in finding one of the few parking spaces left on River Road. The parking spot Pam had found was well past Pancake Pantry, but then getting from one place to another in Gatlinburg meant hoofing it, riding a trolley, or getting your car caught in traffic. Parking wasn't available on the Parkway, so she had only two choices.

Pam got out of her car and walked back in the direction she had driven. River Road. The river part sounded like something made up by a realtor, trying to enhance the value of a piece of property. There were places she could stand in this river and barely get her ankles wet. But the water, the rocks, and the trees were beautiful. She looked over the railing as she made her way to a cross street that ran the short block from River Road uphill to the Parkway. The view along the lesser-traveled River Road was worthy of a photograph and so she took one. She looked up at a hotel that had rooms with balconies overlooking the water. On the Parkway side of River Road were more motel rooms. Pam could already tell that not all hotel and motel rooms in Gatlinburg (or Pigeon Forge) were created equal. But wasn't that true in any vacation place?

+++

There were only a few attractions on River Road, and most places had their own parking lot. Included were motels, hotels, and restaurants. River Road was where people parked if they didn't want to pay to park, were lucky enough to find a place on the street and were willing to walk a few more blocks to get where they were going. The Parkway was where most attractions were.

As Pam took a cross street and crested the hill and arrived on the Parkway she could see a line of cars, heading in both directions. People were getting an early start on their day, and a good number of them were already walking the sidewalks. She looked in each direction and saw no one who looked familiar, not even the stranger she had seen twice at Pancake Pantry.

This time Pam approached Pancake Pantry from the other direction, and the line to get inside was even longer than it was on her previous visits. Of course, that was to be expected. Even vacationers who like to sleep in are more likely to eat breakfast at 9:00 rather than 10:00.

She scanned the line ahead of her. Nothing unusual. Just families with children and couples without children salivating before a good breakfast. A couple of people stepped in line behind her. Casually she turned to look, but they looked no more familiar than those people in front of her.

The nervous woman turned to look across the street and stepped out to look at those approaching Pancake Pantry from each direction. She saw nothing alarming. This time no one had to tap her on the shoulder to get her to move on when the line moved ahead, and at 9:32 she was seated at a table. This time her table was near the back of the restaurant, along a wall.

She cringed when she looked up and saw Carla enter, followed by the strange man who must have stock in the restaurant. One of them entered the restaurant almost immediately after the other, but they didn't sit together. Both sat alone. Pam held her menu up in front of her face, hoping that neither of them would recognize her and approach her. She figured that their presence meant that the kidnapper wouldn't approach her in the restaurant, provided the kidnapper wasn't the strange man. She still felt he was the one, but then the other stranger she had seen there looked more like someone who had served time. But her mind wandered back to the stranger who was there. If he was the one who had sent her the notes, more than likely he hadn't made contact with her because he spotted Carla on her previous visit. While there are many places to eat breakfast in and around Gatlinburg, with many of those having Pancake in the restaurant name, Pam wondered why these two people chose this particular restaurant? Well, Pam knew that Carla chose it because she saw Pam enter the restaurant the day before, but what about the stranger? Pam thought that she got there before him the last time she was there, but what about the first time? Wasn't he there before she was? Did he only return because he saw her there? Surely he wasn't someone who was attracted to her and was afraid to approach her.

Pam had a different server from her previous visits, and of course, the woman didn't recognize her. Still, she tried not to act nervous when the woman approached her table. She ordered and her wait was tougher on her than on her previous visit. She had no front window view to occupy her mind, and she wasn't sure what else to do to hide her nervousness. After an amount of time that seemed longer than it was, her server returned with her food.

Halfway through breakfast, Pam noticed that the stranger had seen her. He looked in her direction and nodded his head. Was that a sign? A sign that they would meet outside after breakfast, or was she to stop by his table on her way out?

Pam finished her meal, which was just as good as before, but, like before, her mind was elsewhere. She made up her mind that she would walk by the man's table on her way out. If he wanted to hand her a note or ask her to sit, she would make it easy on him. After all, she wanted to find Jack, and if this man knew where he was she wanted to get the meeting over with.

As she approached his table, he nodded for her to take a seat.

"You come here often?"

"Only when I'm hungry."

"I hope you don't get hungry at night. This place isn't open."

"So I've noticed."

"You seem to notice a lot."

"I've noticed that this is your favorite place to eat breakfast."

"Yours, too."

"It seems to be, but I'm not always the one who chooses."

"Really? You always seem to be alone. So, who chooses for you?"

"Maybe you do. Do you always write your notes using block letters?"

"Excuse me?"

"Never mind. So, why are you here in Gatlinburg?"

"Vacation. Isn't that why you're here?"

"It is. So, what do you do?"

"Do?"

"You know. Like work."

"Oh, I'm a photographer."

"I mean to make money."

"I have a paper route."

"This is the second time I've seen you here. So who's delivering your papers?"

"My cousin. He needs the money. He lost one of his paper routes."

"And you don't need the money?"

"No. I received a lot of tips for Christmas. It allowed me to take this vacation. Two weeks."

"I'm impressed. Your customers must like you."

"They adore me."

"Well, I'm not sure I do. And I'm married."

"So am I. So where's your husband?"

"So, where's your wife?"

"There weren't enough tips for both of us to come. So, where's your husband?"

"You might know that better than I."

"I'm impressed. A lesser woman would have said 'than me.'"

"And a lesser man wouldn't have asked a woman he didn't know to sit at his table."

"I think nosiness is a trait many paper boys have."

"I think it's been a long time since you were a boy."

"How long has it been since you've seen your husband?"

"As I said, you might know better than I."

"Are you in some kind of trouble?"

"Are you some kind of helper?"

"I'm handy around the house, and in finding lost husbands."

"I think you need to go back to taking pictures and delivering newspapers."

"As you wish, but if you need any help, I'm always around."

"I can tell. I think I'd be happier if you weren't around quite so much."

"Now my feelings are hurt. Okay, this didn't go as well as I hoped. But maybe I'll see you around."

"Maybe I'll try someplace new next time."

"Maybe I will, too. But let me tell you, there's a reason those other places don't have long lines out the door."

"Maybe they have more seating inside."

"And maybe the food isn't as good as it is here."

"Is that all you have for me?"

"You're a tough one to figure out. First, you act like I have leprosy, and then you act like you want to get to know me better. Now, which is it?"

"Let me draw it out for you. I received a note when I got back to our chalet yesterday to meet someone at this restaurant at 10:00. Now, are you that person?"

"No, and it's after 10:00. It looks like you've been stood up. If the note was left by a man, it wasn't a man who has seen you."

"Well, this person is kind of shy. Didn't sign his or her name. But this person knows I'm married, so I wasn't expecting someone to hit on me."

"Well, I wasn't hitting on you. But let me tell you, the fact that you're married won't stop some men from trying. But the reason I stopped you is to see if you need some

112

help. You look like you have something on your mind, and it doesn't appear to be that you just won the lottery."

"I must have one of those faces where I always look like I'm worried about something. The server I had yesterday told me the same thing. Well, if you don't have anything to tell me, then I guess I'm on my way."

"Have it your way. But if you are in trouble, maybe I can help you."

"I'll keep that in mind."

"Please do. I'm around a lot, so just signal and I'll come running."

"As I said, I'll keep that in mind. Goodbye."

20

Pam walked outside and just stood there, right in front of the restaurant. Was that guy the kidnapper, or was he what he said? Well, she was sure that he didn't earn his living from a paper route. But was he a photographer, and someone who just happened to notice that she looked worried? But then again the man had a playful and mocking manner when they talked, which wasn't much different than the notes and text she received.

Pam looked across the street, down the street, and up the street and didn't see anyone waving a ransom note. She was told to enjoy herself, so she turned to check out the Village Shops adjacent to the Pancake Pantry. Later she would check out the Hillbilly Golf place the kidnapper suggested, just in case he was there, or left her a note on Hole Number 9. The shops were set back, off the street, and the miniature golf course was up a hill. Both of those were better places for someone to accost her.

No sooner did Pam think of being accosted than someone grabbed her by her right arm and spun her around.

"Who was that guy?"

"Carla, it's so good to see you, too. How was your breakfast?"

"Don't how was your breakfast me! Who was that guy? You seeing someone on the side, noticed that I was in there, and had to change your plans?"

"Listen, if you prefer eating here, I can go somewhere else tomorrow. I just don't like you accusing me of something after breakfast each morning. It's not good for my digestion."

"Does Jack know about this guy?"

"I doubt it. I don't even know about this guy. I don't even have any idea what his name is."

"Okay. So, let's try this again. Where's Jack?"

"When I left him, he was tied up. Couldn't get away to join me."

"So, did you two have words?"

"Something like that. But I plan to patch things up when I see him."

"So, he left you?"

"Well, we're not together right now, but I assume we'll be home together if that's what you mean. Are you interested in him for yourself?"

"I'm interested in him because of my job."

"You wouldn't happen to know where he is, would you?"

"Me? How would I know? He doesn't hang out in town as you do."

"Well, it looks like you can't help me and I can't help you. It's nice seeing you again, but sometimes I like you better when you're not around."

"And sometimes I'll be around and find out what you're up to."

"Well, listen, it's been fun, but I have to go, and let's not do this again. I'm going this way. Why don't you try going a different way."

+++

Pam walked away and walked over to the candy store next to the Pancake Pantry. She glanced over her shoulder and saw that Carla was just standing there, not walking off in the other direction, but not following her.

There is no prettier area in downtown Gatlinburg than The Village Shops. Twenty-seven unique shops, around the exterior, with brick walkways, benches, wrought-iron fences, flowers, trees, and a park-like setting in the middle. Pam walked underneath a brick archway that signaled the entrance to The Village shops. Each shop was unique, none attractive to everyone, but each one attractive to a good number of people. The brick paths led this way and that, and signs pointed to each of the shops, signs like you might see in some amusement parks, with a European feel. Boutiques, eateries, galleries, Pam studied them all. One shop had nothing but spices. Another sold socks of every type imaginable. Still another sold cheeses, and a fourth sold honey. Pam took a little over an hour, looked through most of the shops. Even if everything had turned up roses for Pam, it wasn't a day for buying. If that happened, it would be just before leaving for home, and she did see a few paintings that would look good on some of her walls at home, particularly one or two she found in the Thomas Kinkade gallery. Well, she did make one purchase. She couldn't resist the donuts at The Donut Friar, and traumatized or not, those donuts wouldn't make it all the way home. If things worked out, she would be back to buy some more to take home, and maybe some of the delicious candy at another shop, too.

No one confronted Pam while she was looking through any of the shops in The Village, so when she walked back out onto the Parkway, she looked this way and that and saw no one who wanted to spend time with her.

The note Pam received mentioned Hillbilly Golf, an attraction several blocks away, so she opted to take a trolley rather than walk all that way. She stopped a woman and asked her if she knew which trolley headed up and down the parkway. A few minutes later, she stepped down off the trolley, saw the building where she would pay to play miniature golf, and when no one motioned for her to come their way, she stepped up and bought a ticket to take the tram up the hill to play eighteen holes. There were racks of putters of various lengths and weights. She tried a few while she waited for the tram to come back from taking up another group. She selected one that felt good in her hands and walked over to wait for the tram. If needed, the putter would be good to ward off attackers. She rode the tram to the top, got off, and found two courses, one to her left, one to her right. She chose the one on the left because there was no one on the first hole. The previous group had chosen the other course. She tried to enjoy herself, even wrote down her score on each hole, even though she played eighteen holes alone. While she played, she kept her eyes open for strangers with an agenda and notes that might have been left for her. A few minutes later she had turned in a respectable score, and left without seeing either of her friends from breakfast, or anyone else who wanted to make her acquaintance.

Twice Pam had been lured away from her vacation paradise, without anyone showing up to accost her. She was tired of someone making her plans for her, just so he or she could leave her a note inviting her to take off on some other wild-goose chase. So, as she stood there contemplating what to do next, she decided to go back to her vehicle and leave the hamlet of Gatlinburg behind. She planned to check out the cabin where she left her husband.

Her Sequoia was even farther away than the Pancake Pantry, so she walked across the street to take a trolley back to the middle of town. She got off by the Aquarium and walked up River Road to where she had parked. When she was a couple of blocks past the Aquarium, the crowd on the sidewalk thinned. Like before, she took her time and looked over the railing at the river. There were few people on River Road, and most of them who had parked there wouldn't return until they were leaving town to go back to where they were staying.

As she walked, Pam hung her head and thought about her predicament. She was so engrossed in her thoughts that she almost passed her car.

"Isn't this one yours?" she heard someone off to the side say.

She looked over and noticed the stranger from breakfast. He smiled at her, hoping to disarm her. It did no good.

"So, you make me run all over town when you could have told me what you wanted at the Pancake Pantry. Okay, let's hear it. What do you want me to do?"

"The same thing I told you at breakfast. Tell me what's wrong. Maybe I can help you."

"You're persistent. I'll say that much for you. So, how did you know where I parked?"

"I'm staying at a hotel that overlooks the Little Pigeon River. I was out on my balcony this morning when you walked by the first time. I guessed that your coming from this direction meant that you were parked up here."

"And?"

"And I decided to come up here and wait for you."

"That's not the *and* I meant. Look around. My car isn't the only one parked on this street, and I don't think every car other than mine has been replaced by another car since breakfast, so how did you figure out which car is mine?"

"I used to be a Boy Scout."

"I have no idea whether you were ever a Boy Scout or not, but I do know there's no badge for identifying cars, so out with it. I'm getting tired of your butting in on my business. So, either tell me what you want or get out of my life."

"The woman does have something on her mind. Trust me. I really can help you."

"And I have a phone, so I can call the police. And a man is standing over there watching us, so it wouldn't be good for you to hit me over the head right now."

The stranger laughed.

"Okay, I give up. I guess you're not going to trust me."

"Not in this lifetime."

"Not even if I tell you that I earned the good conduct medal in the third grade."

"Listen, you might not be a bad guy, but I don't need you in my life right now."

"I think you do, but as you wish. Well, goodbye. I'll see you at breakfast in the morning in case you change your mind."

With that, he walked off before Pam could say another word. Who was this guy? Was he a kidnapper who was trying to gain her trust, a kind-hearted soul who wanted to help her, or some guy with an angle.

Pam waited until she was sure he wasn't parked nearby, then got in her vehicle and took off. She took the first left, then took the next left and got in a long line of traffic on the Parkway, heading through town, back in the direction she left early that morning.

21

Pam sat in traffic, as a large group of people crossed the street a few cars ahead of her. It didn't do to get in a hurry in Gatlinburg. Those who were in a hurry didn't go through town to get to the other side. She had already learned the locals knew which ways to go to get around most of the traffic. And anyone with a GPS knows that there's a bypass around Gatlinburg that leads from the side of Gatlinburg closest to Pigeon Forge to the Great Smoky Mountain National Park.

Motionless, Pam studied the shops on the right-hand side of the street. One in particular interested her. They sold memorabilia of many of the stars from the past. Elvis. Lucy. Marilyn. Audrey Hepburn, and several other people who were famous before she was born. If someone was a big enough name, popular many years ago and still popular today, there was a good chance you could find things there with their picture on it. Lunch boxes. Posters. What have you. Pam made a note of where the shop was located, then drove on as the traffic in front of her started to move. A few minutes later she passed Hillbilly Golf, where she had gotten a couple of holes in one even with the state her mind was in. The miniature golf course is one of the few places in Gatlinburg that has a small parking lot next to the attraction. But that is probably because the golf course is on the edge of town and not in the middle of town.

A Smoky Mountain Mystery

With each block she drove the traffic decreased, her speed increased, and soon she was away from Gatlinburg and on her way to the rundown cabin where she had left her husband. The scenery she passed was beautiful, but Pam was too nervous to notice. Her mind was on her husband and finding out if he was indeed at that cabin, or if someone did kidnap him after she left. She tried to think of all the possibilities she might encounter once she arrived. Maybe Jack was still there and nothing had changed. Maybe he had gotten loose, realized what she had done to him, and chose that avenue to get even with her. Maybe someone had tried to locate Jack and was using Pam to find him. After all, he had told her that he didn't trust his business partner, Bernie. And then, there was the obvious possibility. Someone had followed her, taken Jack after she left him, and had plans that included her. But what had she done that had bothered someone so much that they wanted to cause her harm?

Pam quit thinking about her problems and started looking for her turnoff. A couple of minutes later she recognized the road, put on her turn signal, slowed down, and made her turn. From that point on, each turn onto a new road would be at a higher elevation, and each one more remote than the previous one.

Pam remembered that a few feet after she turned off the main road onto the first of the isolated mountain roads there was a house with a gravel drive in front and the back. She had never seen a car there, and if there was none there this time she had a plan. She turned onto the road and looked quickly. There was no car there, probably hadn't been one there for a while. She doubted if anyone lived in the house, although it was in much better shape than the place she was headed. She thought it belonged to someone who didn't use it as much as they used to.

Pam looked in her rearview mirror, saw no one. So, she turned onto the gravel drive and eased back behind the small house. The gravel consisted of small pieces, like pea gravel, not large chunks, so it was easier for her to manip- ulate her SUV without sliding or sending gravel flying this way and that. She stopped behind the house and waited to see if anyone else turned behind her. A minute later, as- sured that she had no escort or entourage, she pulled back onto the road and drove up the mountain.

The steep incline was enough for Pam to realize that some of these roads didn't get a lot of winter traffic. The incline also caused Pam to have to slow down. There were trees everywhere, except on the road. They seemed to grow like kudzu. They were everyplace, including hiding each new road until she was almost upon it. Pam remembered that the road she was looking for was near the top of the mountain. The fact that it was unmarked meant that she had to pay close attention to where she was going. It would be only her third time to go there. The road was relatively flat, bearing some resemblance to the roads at Cade's Cove. Pam thought back to the trip she and Jack had made there just a few days before. The way her life was going it seemed like a lot longer ago than a few days. The road she was look- ing for actually went slightly downhill, although, in reality, it didn't go much of anywhere as far as Pam could tell. Sev- eral minutes later, she saw the dilapidated cabin a hundred feet or so ahead of her. She stopped, watched, and listened. As far as she could tell, there was no one within a mile of her. She glanced in her rear-view mirror. Nothing there, either. Not even a deer, or a bear, or someone who got side- tracked while walking the Appalachian Trail.

With the doors of her vehicle still locked, she eased on down the road, ready to hit the gas if someone popped out of the cabin or from behind a tree. She stopped directly in front of the cabin, looked, rolled down her window and listened. There was nothing. But whether there was some- one inside or not, she didn't expect to find a welcoming party waiting for her on the small front porch. She didn't know where the road went, but she did remember the route she had taken to get there, so she drove on past the cabin until she got to a place where she could turn around. The road was still narrow enough that she had to pull up and back a few times before she was headed back in the direction from which she came.

Once again, she stopped in front of the cabin. She felt in her large bag to make sure she still had the gun. It was there. She opened the door of her car and slowly stepped out onto the road. She stood there a moment. The sky didn't darken. Well, she figured it didn't. She couldn't see much sky. Too many trees for that. No black cat crossed her path, so she took her first step toward the cabin, her bag in hand.

Halfway there she stopped, looked left, right, at the cabin, and even turned around and looked behind her. There were no dangerous beings or endangered species near her in the woods. No grinning kidnapper was sitting in the driver's seat of her vehicle, no one coming at her wearing a hockey mask or carrying a chainsaw. It was safe as far as she could tell.

Pam couldn't stand there forever. Either she needed to check inside that cabin or get back in her vehicle and drive away. She knew that if she didn't open that cabin door and look inside that whether or not Jack was still inside would continue to torment her. So, she convinced herself to do what she didn't want to do but knew that it was what she must do. Slowly she walked toward the cabin. She stepped up onto the first porch step, stopped and listened again. Nothing. She took the second step, and then the third. The squeak that emanated from the old step permeated through her body. She stood there, motionless as if being still made any difference. It was only a couple of more steps to the cabin. When the squeaking step didn't lead to a reaction, she walked over, reached into her bag and grabbed the gun, pointed it at the door with her right hand, reached for the doorknob with her left, and turned it until it opened. Then she shoved the door so hard that it hit the cabin wall.

22

Pam never got inside to see if her husband was there or not. As soon as she shoved the door open, a board came down from above, hit her in the forehead, and knocked her back. If the board had been a couple of inches longer, it would have broken her nose. She landed on the edge of the porch and slid down the steps on her back. The blow was enough that it knocked Pam out. She lay there, unconscious, but not for long. In less than a minute, someone had scooped her up, carried her inside the cabin, and turned her into a hostage.

Several minutes later, Pam woke up groggy. It was a few seconds before she became aware of where she was. Well, it was doubtful that Pam knew where she was, but after a couple of minutes of assessing the situation, she realized that she was somewhere, seated on an uncomfortable chair. Something was covering her eyes to where she couldn't see. She had a gag in her mouth. Her hands were bound behind her, and her feet secured together and to the chair on which she sat. Other than that, she was doing okay. Well, okay as long as she didn't count the terrible headache the falling board had given her.

Pam couldn't see, and she couldn't move. But she could smell and the smells she sensed told her she was in the mountains, and it was musty where she was. The only positive smells were the ones she couldn't smell. There was no smell of gasoline. No smell of fire. At least that was something. Not only could she smell, but she could listen, too. And so she did. But she didn't hear anything. Pam heard no footsteps and no rat scurrying across the floor. No cat chasing the rat that wasn't there or using her leg as a scratching post. No dog nipping at her ankles. And no traffic zipping or crawling by outside. But she didn't think her accommodations were so exquisite that she was in a soundproof room.

Not only could she hear, but she could feel, too, if only from her confined position. Still, it was enough to let her know she was inside somewhere, probably in a small room with a wooden floor. Possibly a cabin. Were the kidnappers holding her in their mountain hideout? If so, were they holding Jack in the same place? Maybe in the same room? She listened again. She didn't hear anyone breathing. She hoped that if there was another hostage in the same room she was in that whoever it was was breathing. It didn't bode well for her if they weren't. But then, it didn't bode well for her anyway.

She tried to call out, but could only emit a muffled sound. Still, it was sufficient that anyone nearby could have heard. She was alone. She was sure of that. Was it good or bad that she was alone? She didn't try to call out a second time. She didn't want to choke on her gag. She held her head slightly forward, so the gag wouldn't fall back toward her throat. Could it be that the kidnapper had left her for a while but would soon be back? She contemplated whether or not to try to escape but first wondered from where it was that she had to escape.

Where was she? She ruled out any high-priced Gatlinburg getaway with a scenic overlook. The smell of her surroundings told her the maid hadn't been in for a few months. Even the Bates Motel had clean rooms, each cleaned again after every murder. She wondered if she was in the cabin where she had left her husband. It could be the same place. And what plans did her attacker have for her?

126

She struggled, tried to move. On her second attempt, she was successful. The chair on which she was sitting toppled over and she hit her head a second time, this time against the wooden floor. Only termites were more attracted to wood than her head was. The Richter Scale moment didn't send any spiders crawling across her face. And no one laughed, came to help her to her feet, or kick her in the head. She tried to get up. In her condition that would have been slightly difficult if she hadn't been secured to a chair. But she was able to move herself and the chair. Still, there was nothing about her small change of venue that would be considered progress. She lay there, wondering when her antagonist would be back. Then she wondered if they would be back. Maybe whoever had done this to her planned to leave her there until the next human stumbled across the cabin, entered it, and wondered where those bones came from.

Pam heard a sound outside and let out a guttural sound. Someone had closed a car door. Her attacker was returning. She wasn't sure if that was good or bad. Was whoever it was planning to shoot her, or had he stopped by a drive-thru and brought her something to eat. Suddenly cold fries didn't sound quite so bad. She remained still, listened. She thought someone was approaching her position, but she wasn't sure. Then she was sure. The same step that squeaked when she stepped up onto it squeaked again. Then Pam knew where she was. She wished she had her gun, but whoever tied her up had taken it from her. Most kidnappers do things like that. They don't want you trying to shoot through the duct tape and shooting yourself in the leg instead. Or worse. If they had wanted blood, they would have done that themselves.

Pam wasn't even able to use her hands and feet to protect herself. Well, not unless she was able to spin the chair and take her assailant's legs out from under him. And what good would that do her? It might make him angry, and make him harm her more than he had already done.

Pam lay on the floor, braced herself, and waited. Even when he opened the door she wouldn't know who he was unless he spoke, and she wasn't sure that she would recognize his voice. What if her captor was someone she had never seen?

Finally, he opened the door. He stood there a moment, silent, looking at her. At least she figured he was looking at her. After all, Pam was seated upright when he left. Or was there more than one person? From what she could tell, she had heard only one set of footsteps.

He broke the silence and she knew immediately who her visitor was.

"What in the world happened to you?"

Pam tried to tell from his voice inflection if he meant he had left her in the chair upright, or he was surprised to find her there all trussed up.

"So, you don't need my help. Does that mean you want me to leave again?"

Pam muttered something indistinguishable and contemplated using the chair spin kick.

She felt him come over, bend down toward her. He lifted the chair and sat her upright again. And then the pain hit her. Gentle wasn't a word Pam would have used for the manner her companion used to rip the duct tape from her mouth. As far as she could tell, she still had her lips. And he didn't extricate any teeth as he pulled the handkerchief from her mouth.

"Ouch!"

"Sorry. Do you need my help now, or should I leave you the way I found you?"

"Get me out of this chair!"

"As you wish. Now, it may hurt again. I'm taking this duct tape from your eyes, and it may take some of your hair with it."

This time Pam cried out louder. She felt like head-butting him, but then that isn't something to do to someone who is helping you. He was helping her. Wasn't he?

"Why did you do this to me? What do you want?"

He pulled a knife from his pocket. Pam jumped back, as best she could, almost toppled the chair backward.

"Do you want me to cut all this tape from your hands and feet or not? It's no skin off my teeth. I can just sit here and watch you squirm."

"Just hurry up!"

"It does my heart good when someone is grateful when I come to her rescue."

"So, do you do this often?"

"A little more than the average guy."

"Why do you do it?"

"Weren't you listening? I said it does my heart good."

"You like tying up defenseless women?"

"I don't know. I haven't had to do that yet."

"So you have your accomplice do the dirty work?"

"When are you going to learn that I'm the good guy?"

Pam remained silent while the stranger cut away the duct tape. When he had finished, he helped her to her feet for a moment, steadied her, then motioned for her to take a seat.

"So, are you going to tell me what happened?"

"I don't know. I remember I approached this cabin."

"The one we're in?"

"I don't know. I'll have to see the outside."

"I'm pretty sure it was this cabin. Your SUV is outside."

"So, they didn't take it?"

"So, I'm no longer the bad guy. We're making progress here."

"I'm not sure whether you're the bad guy or not. I just know that someone was prepared for my visit, and something hit me in the head when I opened the door."

"And why did you come to this particular cabin? Surely this isn't where you're staying when you and I aren't having our rendezvous?"

"Of course not."

"So, you just stumbled upon this place?"

"Not exactly. So, are you telling me that you just happened to find me here? It's pretty remote."

"Would you believe this place is on my paper route?"

"If so, they must have stopped delivery when they went on vacation."

"How do you know? Your eyes were covered. How do you know there aren't any newspapers stacked outside?"

"I remember coming here now. And there weren't any newspapers."

"Which takes me back to my question. Why are you at this out of the way place?"

"How do you know the kidnappers didn't bring me here?"

"I don't. But if they did, one of them drove your car and they left in another, or on foot."

"And you still haven't told me how you happened to find me here. It's not like this place is on the way to someplace."

"I doubt if it is. Anyway, I have my ways. And I did find you and set you free."

"But you still have too many secrets. And you want me to trust you?"

"So far, you haven't told me anything. You're kind of mysterious yourself."

"Let's just say that I prefer to work alone."

"Yeah, and look where that has gotten you. So, are you going to tell me anything else about why you're here?"

"Maybe later. Right now I have a splitting headache. I need to get back to where I'm staying."

"Well, you're not in any shape to drive. So, you're going to have to trust me a little bit."

"Fine. Just get me back to my chalet."
"Are you in any position to tell me how to get to it?"
"I think so. Just give me a few minutes."

23

Pam sat, hoping that she would be back to her old self in just a few minutes. The stranger merely stood there and watched her.

"Okay, I think I'm ready."

Pam stood up and immediately sat back down.

"What round did he knock me out in?"

"I don't know. I missed that part. Got caught in traffic. Was it a good fight?"

"Not from my perspective."

"Now if you want to sit a few more minutes, I'm willing to wait."

"No. I'm good."

"I doubt that. Stand up. I'll grab your arm."

Like a newborn colt, Pam got to her feet. Only the stranger's sure hand kept her from toppling over or sinking back down into the chair.

"I don't think you'll remember this day fondly."

"Well, it's not exactly the highlight of my vacation so far. And I don't even know who to complain to about the hospitality."

"You can complain to me. Tell me what happened. I'm all ears."

"Maybe later. I don't want to be stranded where I'm staying. Is it okay if we take my SUV?"

"That might work. After all, you do need someone to stay with you for a while. I'm not a doctor, but you might have suffered a concussion."

"I want to be alone."

"I think Garbo said it better."

"But my English is better. And besides, I don't think anyone beat her over the head not long before she said her line."

"Point taken. Anyway, I'm going to have to stay with you until someone can pick me up."

"So, you do have an accomplice?"

"Accomplice? Am I back to being the bad guy again?"

"Let's just say I'm weighing my options. You might be someone who prefers slow torture."

" I am. But back to the point. I prefer to refer to my ride as a friend, not an accomplice."

"Whatever! Just get me back to my place."

"As you wish, oh grateful one."

Pam was still a little groggy but caused her rescuer to take only one wrong turn. A few minutes later, they returned to the place Pam recognized, and after overcoming her refusal for help, he helped her to the door.

"Well, it looks like you've had a visitor. Someone left you a note. You want me to read it?"

Pam became unnerved when her chauffeur told her she had another note but relaxed somewhat when she saw the envelope didn't match the ones left by the kidnapper.

"I'll read it later. Maybe it's from the kidnapper and it's for my eyes only."

"Let's test the logic of that. Someone ties you up, leaves you for dead, then drives up here and leaves you a note. Makes sense to me."

"Well, somebody left it. And for an out-of-the-way hideaway, a lot of people know about this place."

"Someone must have posted a video on YouTube."

"I'm not in any mood for your jokes, and just because you're trying to be funny doesn't mean that I trust you any more than I did before."

"Listen, if you have some duct tape, I'll be glad to take you back where I found you, and bind you again."

"Now that I'm thinking a little more clearly, how did you find me?"

"Didn't I tell you before? I have my ways."

Pam turned from the man she knew only as the stranger who always seemed to be at Pancake Pantry. She fumbled with the security code that allowed her to open the door. Because Pam's head was still located right in front of the percussion section of the orchestra, and the piece they had just played had repeated parts that included cymbals, it took her a little longer to remember the code than it did before. Once inside the chalet, the stranger removed her shoes, put a pillow under her head, and instructed her to lie down on the couch but not to go to sleep.

"As I said before, I think you' have a concussion. It would be best if I stayed with you for a few hours."

"I'll be fine, just as soon as I get some sleep."

"Okay, stubborn one, but I'll be back in the morning to check on you, and I might drive by from time to time tonight."

"You mean we're not meeting at Pancake Pantry for breakfast?"

"We could always do that. We'll talk about that later. Oh, that reminds me. Is this yours?"

Pam looked at the cell phone.

"Yeah. Where did you find it?"

"Beside the steps. I guess whoever attacked you missed it. Here you go."

After more offers to stay and repeated protests, the stranger left just after receiving a text. A few minutes later, Pam stumbled over and looked out to make sure the stranger had truly left. She saw a vehicle driving away. She guessed it was the man the stranger had called to pick him up. She shut the door, secured it, and stumbled back to the couch to lie down.

She had almost forgotten about the envelope that someone had left on her door. She reached over to the coffee table, grabbed the envelope, and opened it the best she could without ripping the message inside.

Pam,

If you run into the stranger you saw at the Pancake Pantry, don't trust him. I think he's the one who has Jack. He will try to act like he's a friend, and may even say he's with the FBI. And he might even show you proof, which will look authentic.

A Friend

Who had written the note and left it for her? Was the stranger who seemed to have her best interest at heart really with the FBI? Pam didn't know what to make of the note or the stranger, but she knew that someone was playing rough and it was time to alert the authorities. She still had the card the policeman had given her when he came to the cabin. He would know what to do. She reached over, grabbed the card, grabbed her phone, and punched in his number. No one answered. Only an electronic voice asking her to leave a message.

The chalet had a local phone book, so Pam got up off the couch, walked over, picked up the phone book, and sat down again to look up the number of the police department. She punched in the numbers and waited for someone to answer.

"Sevier County Sheriff's Department."

"Sgt. Cletus Culpepper, please."

"I'm sorry. There's no one here by that name. May someone else help you."

"No, I need to speak to Sgt. Culpepper. It's about a matter he and I spoke about before."

"Ma'am, you don't understand. We don't have a Sgt. Cletus Culpepper."

"Yes, you do. I spoke to him. He stopped by the last time I had a police matter, even left me his card. And I saw his car, too. It said Sevier County Sheriff's Department on it, just like the other cars I've seen since we've gotten here."

"Well, I'm sorry. If you think someone was imper- sonating a police officer, we need to know about it."

"No, that's okay. I must be mistaken."

"Well, call us back if you have another matter."

Pam hung up, called the Tennessee State Police. They had never heard of anyone named Cletus Culpepper, either.

Pam knew that something had struck her in the head. Could her head be playing tricks on her? She lay back down, not sure whether to be terrified or not. She only knew that her husband was missing, his secretary was in the area, some stranger kept turning up wanting to help her, and the only policeman she had met might not be a policeman. She felt for her gun, then remembered that it was gone. Either the stranger hadn't given it back to her, or whoever had tied her up in the cabin had taken it. All she had for protection was the self-defense class she had taken, and that wasn't much help to her the last time she needed it.

24

Pam's world was spinning around. When she had gotten up that morning she had no idea she would be bound and gagged, left in a dilapidated cabin, rescued, left a note by someone warning her, and find out that the person she felt she could trust the most might be the person she could trust the least.

She remembered something she had heard once about a concussion, just in case a concussion was what she had. It was a good thing to stay awake, and she remembered that a friend of hers had a concussion once, and while some of the symptoms remained for a while, her friend felt most of the way back to normal in a couple of hours. She had no idea if what had happened to her had happened a couple of hours before or not, but there was a good chance it had been that long. She had no way of knowing how long she was a prisoner in that cabin and wasn't even sure how long it had been since the stranger had found her. But then she knew she hadn't been knocked out overnight, so she tried to reconstruct her day. It had to have been mid- or late afternoon when she arrived at the cabin, so, yes, it had been at least two hours.

But whatever the case, she planned to stay awake for a while for a couple of reasons. One was in case someone, friend or foe, visited her. Of course, how was she to know who was a friend and who was a foe? Particularly since she learned that the man she thought was a policeman

137

probably wasn't a cop and could have been someone trying to harm her. Surely his charade meant that he planned to harm Jack, her, or both of them. Would he have reacted differently if she hadn't greeted him with a gun? The second reason she planned to stay awake was to evaluate what had happened to her to see if she could better understand her situation.

For the time being Pam would forget about anything that happened before getting to the cabin earlier that day and think about the nightmare that happened there. Of course, she didn't know what happened there. She would have to guess.

Pam closed her eyes, tried to concentrate, focus on what happened to her earlier that day. As she tried to think, it seemed like she was better able to do so than she had been when she first arrived back at her chalet. She tried to picture the moment she had arrived at the cabin. Had she gotten even a glimpse of someone when she pushed open the door, before whatever it was knocked her out? She didn't think so. As far as she could figure, someone had rigged a board to come crashing down and knock her out as soon as she opened the door. And she was fairly certain that no one was there when she came to. But they had to have been somewhere nearby when it happened, or arrived shortly thereafter, to have trussed her up. So, who could have done it? Could it have been her husband? Could he have escaped and lured her there? Or did someone discover her husband there and lure her back to the cabin to do something to her, too? If so, who could it have been? Was it the stranger who appeared to be so helpful, the man the note warned her about? Could it have been the man she thought was with the local police department, a man no one in the police department had heard of? Or how about Carla, her husband's secretary? Could Carla and Jack be in it together? Or what about Bernie, Jack's partner? Could he and Carla have caused Jack to disappear and wanted to get rid of her as a possible witness? Maybe they had murdered Jack. Or was it someone she didn't know existed?

She wasn't getting anywhere with adventure number one, so it was time to move on to when she returned to the chalet. Who could have left the note? It didn't make sense that it was the same person who left her tied up in the cabin. Whoever did that and left must have thought that there was no way to escape. Unless whoever it was returned to the cabin when the stranger was there and saw that someone had come to her aid. If they hurried they could have gotten from there to the chalet in time to leave a note and get away before she and the stranger returned. So, who left the note? Was it someone who knew something about the stranger? If so, were they afraid he would harm her, or afraid he would help her? As Pam recalled each time she met him, the only thing that constituted a red flag was that the man always seemed to know what was going on. It was like he was one step ahead of her. But he acted like he wanted to help her. But did someone know the stranger Pam met at Pancake Pantry was someone she should avoid? As far as she knew, only Carla knew about the stranger, and Pam doubted that Carla would have a clue whether or not the man had anything to do with the FBI. Of course, there was a good chance that whoever left the note didn't have a clue whether or not the stranger could even spell FBI. They merely had a reason to see him out of the picture. And the only way Pam would know whether or not the person who left the note meant her harm, or help from a distance, would be to find out the identity of that person. What about the handwriting, and the envelope? The note Carla had given to Pam's server didn't have an envelope, and this envelope wasn't the same as the one the so-called kidnapper had left twice before. Plus, this one was typed. That alone was enough to tell Pam that the person's actions were premeditated. No one carries a printer with them in their car. Did that mean that whoever wrote and left the note now had access to a computer and a printer, but didn't have one when he left the first note? Or could it be that whoever left it was afraid that Pam would recognize the handwriting? But she wasn't sure she would recognize anyone's handwriting, except for Jack's. Could Jack have gotten away and left the note when he couldn't find her at the chalet? But if it was Jack, why didn't he leave it inside, and why didn't he sign the note? Jack could have forgotten the security code, thus the reason he left it on the door. But it was doubtful he had forgotten his own name but remembered who the bad guy was. But was the note ever on the door? It had to be. Otherwise, it would have had to have come from the stranger, and he wasn't dumb enough to say to her, "Don't trust me." Well, unless he thought that would make her trust him because nothing else he had said or done had turned the trick.

But why would the FBI be interested in her? There wasn't a reason. But they could be interested in Jack, provided Jack had done something wrong. Or could it be Bernie who had done something wrong, and Jack had contacted the FBI and Bernie had found out about it? But then the stranger didn't look or act anything like anyone she had ever heard was connected with the FBI. At least not the ones she had seen on TV. FBI agents are more serious than the 1960's IBMers, and IBMers dress like nerds with taste. And they're more serious than a funeral director. Surely, this guy couldn't be an FBI agent, but did someone think he was? Or was that designed to have Pam think more about the stranger than she thought about the person who left the note, who may or may not be a stranger?

Pam hadn't even gotten to the point yet where she wondered how the policeman who wasn't a policeman fit into the situation. But she knew that someone who has been hit over the head doesn't need to be contemplating all the strange and bad things that had happened that day.

Pam changed her focus. She wished she had Google handy. Was it good for someone who had suffered a concussion to eat? She just knew she was hungry, and a concussion wasn't a cold or a fever, and she couldn't even remember which of those she was to feed and which one to starve. After a few more seconds of muddled thought, she decided she wasn't the one she was to starve, so she rose to her feet. That was a good sign. The room didn't seem to be spinning. The kitchen looked like it was in the same place she remembered it to be. She recognized the refrigerator and the stove. But cooking anything on the stove was out. She just wanted to fix something quick and lie back down. She would put off any more thinking of her situation until after she had eaten, and maybe even until the next morning, provided she was still alive.

25

The Ninth Day

Pam awoke the next morning still feeling a little "funny". She lay there, contemplating her situation from a different perspective.

If I think of each of the people I've seen since I arrived here, maybe I can have a better idea which one did this to me.

Pam felt the best place to start was with Jack. She had received a phone call from a private detective, who said her mother hired him and he felt her husband was trying to kill her. Well, the first part of that equation was true. Her mother did hire the man. But did that mean that her husband was trying to murder her? What reason would he have? Was there another woman? If so, it must be Carla, but if so, and Carla was in on what was going on, Carla was a terrific actress. But before Pam got to Carla, she needed to look at her husband, think of where he might be, because he certainly wasn't in the dilapidated cabin where she left him. As far as Pam could tell, there were only a few possibilities as to where Jack could be. One, he escaped and was hiding from Bernie, or whoever Bernie had hired to murder him. Maybe Jack couldn't remember what had happened and thought Bernie was responsible. Pam remembered that Jack had said that he couldn't trust Bernie or something like that. But she would get to Bernie later. She was still thinking about Jack. So, two, Jack was on his own and was trying to get even with her. Or, if the private detective was right, murder her. But then maybe Jack didn't remember that she was the one who put him in the cabin. Maybe he felt that both of them were attacked and someone had kidnapped Pam and left him there. It wasn't as if Pam had knocked him out as someone had done to her. Well, she had, but not with a blunt instrument. She used ether. She wasn't sure what ether does to someone's memory. But anyway, maybe his thinking wasn't muddled. Maybe he knew who was responsible for his being left there. So, was Jack responsible for Pam's ordeal in the rustic cabin, and if so, had he planned to leave her there until she died, planned to release her after a certain time, or murder her? Pam had to admit, even if Jack knew she was responsible for his incarceration, he didn't know whether she had planned to come back and release him after a certain time. Maybe he thought the worst. Maybe he didn't.

So, had Jack escaped, with or without help? And if he did have help, was that help in the form of the bogus policeman, or Carla? Pam guessed someone could have stumbled upon him as they hiked through the woods, but the chance of that happening was slim. But then that thought made her wonder how the stranger from Pancake Pantry had found her in the cabin. It would have been almost as unlikely that he stumbled upon her as it would have been that someone discovered Jack the prisoner. So, the stranger either followed her and she wasn't aware of it, or he was the one who imprisoned her. At least Pam didn't see any other possibility.

Pam's thoughts kept leaving Jack before she was ready to move on. Where was Jack? Was he free and on his own? Was he a prisoner of someone at another location, or had someone murdered him? Each time she thought of murder it reminded her that Jack was worried about what

Bernie might want to do to him. Could the fake policeman have been working for Bernie, who sent him to murder Jack, and possibly Pam, too?

Pam was no further along in solving her dilemma than she had been the night before. She wished she had seen who was responsible for her headache. But then maybe if she had, she wouldn't have been alive to talk about it. That made her think that whoever had rigged the apparatus to fall and hit her in the head wasn't at the cabin when it happened. Could it be that that person had taken Jack somewhere Pam didn't know about and had hidden him so that she couldn't find him? If so, more than likely it wasn't far from where she had left him. Because whoever rigged the contraption to knock Pam out must have known she wouldn't be unconscious forever. Unless they thought the blow would have been enough to kill her, which she doubted. So, whoever was responsible for her attack needed to get back before she regained consciousness. But then she realized that even after she regained consciousness, she wouldn't have been any match for an adversary.

Pam thought about everyone she had encountered in Gatlinburg, plus the people who might have followed Jack there. Well, she ruled out the servers at Pancake Pantry. She didn't suspect any of them were responsible for what had happened to Jack or her. But there was the fake cop, the stranger who acted like he wanted to be her friend, Carla, and maybe Bernie provided Bernie had followed them to Tennessee.

After a few minutes, Pam gave up. All of that thinking made her head hurt. It was time to decide what she planned to do that day.

First was breakfast. Did she plan to drive to Gatlinburg, or fix breakfast herself? She didn't like either choice. Then she remembered the stranger had driven her back to the chalet. But did he give her the key to the SUV after they returned? She couldn't remember him doing it, but then she couldn't remember a lot of things. She slowly rose from the bed, hoping that doing so wouldn't give her a splitting headache. It still felt funny, but it wasn't what you would call a headache.

She checked her phone to see the time. 8:14. She noticed that no one had called her and left a message. She walked slowly to the living room, grabbed her purse, and riffled through it. No keys. No keys on the counter, either. It did her no good to have her vehicle if she didn't have a key to start it. She picked up the pace and hurried to the door and opened it, without realizing she hadn't dressed. She quickly used the door for cover when she noticed that not only was her SUV where they had left it the night before but that the stranger's vehicle was parked right behind it. And when he saw her he started smiling. He reached down and held up her keys, dangled them to where she could see them. She couldn't tell from his bemused look whether his smile was because she wasn't dressed for company, that he had the keys and she didn't, or that he was glad to see that she was okay. Unsure, she gave him a quick wave, shut the door, and hurried off to get dressed.

26

Pam thought about the stranger while she hurried to get dressed. She didn't want him walking in on her, wasn't sure whether he could do that or not. Did he know the security code? She didn't think so, but she wasn't sure of anything anymore. She also wasn't sure that she could trust him. As far as she knew, he hadn't done anything to harm her. At least not while she was conscious. And the only thing he could have done anyway was rig the board that came down and knocked her out. She wondered how hard that would be and how long it would take someone to do it. Was Jack handy enough with tools to do something like that? She doubted it. Well, she wasn't sure. She merely knew that he didn't have a workshop. Something like that didn't interest him. But enough about Jack. She had to finish getting dressed before the stranger barged in on her, or take so long that he might drive off again with her keys. Maybe he had only kept the key to keep her from driving off somewhere in her condition.

She hurried back to the door, opened it, and held out her hand like she was expecting him to bring her keys to her. Then she turned away from the slightly opened door and walked over to take a seat.

A few seconds later she heard his approaching footsteps. She looked up and saw that he was carrying a large bag.

"What's that?"

"Breakfast. I wasn't sure that you were up to going to Pancake Pantry today, and I didn't know if you had enough food for two, so I brought a few things."

"I don't remember inviting you to breakfast."

"I understand. A lot of people have a faulty memory after a knock on the head like you had. So, I'll pretend you said 'thank you' and I'll start breakfast."

"You know I don't know much about you. I'm not in the habit of inviting strangers to breakfast."

"And I'm not in the habit of helping defenseless women all tied up in an out-of-the-way cabin."

"I thought you told me you excelled at that. So, tell me something about yourself."

"I'm hungry. Is that enough? So where's the skillet? You do like bacon and eggs, don't you? And I fix a mean sausage gravy and homemade biscuits."

"And what if my husband comes in while you're here?"

"I'll make enough for three."

"Don't you think he might think it odd that you are here so early in the morning?"

"No odder than I think it is that he's not here now. Now, let's try this again. Where's the skillet? And is there anything you don't like for breakfast?"

"It's in the dishwasher, and I don't like strangers for breakfast."

"It's a good thing I've been around enough times that I'm no longer a stranger. Otherwise, I might think I'm not wanted."

Pam sighed.

"If you'd quit yapping and start breakfast we might get something to eat around here."

"That's my girl."

"I'm not your girl. I'm my husband's wife."

"That's just a figure of speech. I remember you're married, and if you've noticed, I haven't done anything out of the way."

+++

Pam watched as the stranger fixed breakfast. She had to admit he was handsome. She shook her head to shake away any thoughts of the stranger and how he looked. She was married. At least she was still married unless someone had murdered her husband, and even if that had happened, she was in no frame of mind to hook up with anyone else. But he was handsome.

But what else was he? Was he a friend or foe? He appeared to want to help her, but was that to disarm her? Could it be that he knew who she was and that her husband had a lot of money? And if so, did he know that she wouldn't have control of the business unless both her husband and Bernie died, and then she would still have to split it with Roz, Bernie's wife? She didn't want any part of that. There was something about Roz that said, "you can't trust me," but then wasn't that how Jack had begun to feel about Bernie?

Pam's eyes shifted from the stranger to the note someone had delivered saying that he would claim to be FBI, but he wasn't and wasn't to be trusted. But was that true? So far she had been around him a few times, and he hadn't tried to convince her that he was FBI. And it wasn't as if she could call the FBI and ask, "Do you have an agent such-and-such?" She didn't even know his name, or whoever he claimed to be, because so far he hadn't claimed to be anyone.

She turned and looked at him. The bacon and eggs were done, and he was busy making gravy.

"You know you haven't even told me your name."

"No, I haven't."

"Why not? Are you wanted for something?"

"Gee, I hope so. A man just can't feel that good about himself unless he's wanted for something."

"You know what I mean."

"No, I'm not wanted for anything in the sense you mean, and you can call me Jake."

"In other words, that's not your real name."

"Does it matter? It would make me feel good if someone allowed me to call them a name that only I could call them."

"So, why don't I call you Brucie? It could be my name for you."

"If that's what you want, but I don't think of myself as a hairdresser."

"Me, either. I was thinking more of a criminal type."

"You know I still have time to put arsenic in these eggs."

"Go ahead. I'll let you try them first and see if you put enough in."

"Is that what you gave to your husband? Arsenic?"

"How did you know? It was the Smith & Wesson brand."

"Somehow I don't think you'd know the difference between Smith & Wesson and Glock."

"You'd be surprised. So, is Glock your weapon of choice?"

"Sorry, I don't tell a woman personal stuff like that until the second time we've had breakfast together."

"Doesn't Pancake Pantry count as having breakfast together?"

"Nope. We didn't eat at the same table."

+++

The banter ended when the stranger sat the breakfast on the table. Pam got up from where she was sitting on the couch and joined him at the table. She was surprised when he bowed his head to pray before he ate, but then she figured that some psychopaths pray before murdering their quarry.

+++

The stranger ate breakfast with Pam, saw that she was doing better, gave her the key to the Sequoia, and left. He still hadn't given her his name, and she wasn't going to call him Brucie and refrained from calling him Jake, either, because she doubted that was his name.

While she was feeling better, she had no plans to leave the chalet that day, even though it was a pleasant day. She stepped outside, walked up the road, and looked both ways. She saw nothing out of the way.

She decided to kill two birds with one stone. She got on the Internet to occupy her mind and checked out *The Lexington Herald-Leader* to see if she found her husband or his business partner mentioned there. When her search turned up empty and she had caught up on the news back home, she Googled her husband, and again came up with nothing out of the ordinary.

It was time for her to call Jack's office, disguise her voice, and ask for him. When someone answered, she went into her act.

"Mr. Archer, please."

"I'm sorry, but Mr. Archer isn't in at the moment."

"Do you know when you're expecting him?"

"I can't tell you that. Can someone else help you?"

"I guess I can speak to Carla, his secretary."

"I'm sorry, but she's on vacation this week."

"Is Mr. Archer also on vacation?"

"That I can't tell you."

"Well, is Mr. Carlucci there."

"I'm sorry, but he isn't available, either."

"Thank you."

+++

Pam waited over an hour and then called back.

"Gladys Phelps, please."

"One moment, please."

"Hey, Gladys, this is Pam Archer. Jack left a couple of days ago on business and hasn't returned. Has he by any chance been in the office?"

"That's news to me. I heard the two of you were on vacation."

"We are, but he had something urgent. You know Jack. Always having to work."

"Boy do I know that. I was surprised to hear that he took some time off. I don't think anyone here knew about it ahead of time, except I guess Bernie did. I thought maybe the four of you went somewhere together. I believe Roz left just after the two of you, and Bernie left a day later, said he'd be gone for a few days."

"Who knows? Maybe the two of them are hunkered down somewhere discussing business. You never know. Is Carla there?"

"No, she's on vacation, too. I think you left Thursday or Friday. Well, I didn't think she was scheduled for a vacation right now, but on Monday I get this e-mail saying she's on vacation for a few days. Didn't even say when she'd be back. Boy, I wish I could just up and go on vacation like that. The funny thing is that no one around here knew that any of you were headed on vacation. "

"I didn't know the others were going, and we just decided at the last minute. I caught Jack in a weak moment and he agreed to go. Well, it sounds like everyone else is gone. You might as well take off, too."

"I'd love to, but somebody has to run things around here. Actually, most everyone else is in. If I hear from your husband I'll tell him he needs to check in."

"Yeah, he usually does, although sometimes it's not until late at night. Listen, I'll let you go. Thanks, and take care."

+++

Pam too thought it was funny that everyone up and decided to go on vacation at the same time. She wondered if any of the other missing suspects had anything to do with where Jack might be or anything that had happened to her.

+++

Pam no longer felt as safe as she had before, but when nothing had happened by late afternoon she slipped off her clothes and sank in the hot tub. The time she spent there was the most relaxed she had been in days, even though there was no gun nearby to protect her in case someone came charging through the front door. Nothing happened and after a few minutes of soaking her worries away, she stepped out, dried off, and plopped down and leaned back in a comfortable chair. No one invaded her privacy except for an occasional bird in flight and none of them paid any attention to her. She was beginning to feel safe again.

27

Pam had never been in her current position, and she didn't know anyone else who had. What does a woman who is supposed to be on vacation with her husband do when her husband disappears? And what does a woman who has been told her husband plans to murder her do? Should she report all that had happened to the local police? On the surface that made sense, but then she couldn't tell them about her husband's disappearance without telling them about the cabin, and she couldn't tell them about the cabin without implicating herself. There was no way to lie about stumbling upon the cabin and have them believe her tale. By the same token, she didn't feel she could go back home, either. Doing so would take just as much of a leap. So, until their time in the chalet was up, she felt she had two choices. She could either stay holed up in the mountains or act like a normal person would while on vacation. After thinking about it for a couple of minutes, she decided to act like a normal person. While the Hatfield & McCoy show seemed so long ago to her, it had only been a little over a week. But the people she met there and the suggestions they gave her on how to enjoy herself had been good ones so far. One woman had told her to make sure and spend at least a half-day on what many called the Craft Loop. She liked shopping as much as any woman. Well, maybe not that much, but she loved to shop, and the Craft Loop consisted of over 100 small stores along a lopsided oval-like couple of roads. She couldn't check all of them out in a half-day, but she would shop until she grew tired. And so her plans were made for the next day.

+++

The Tenth Day

Pam got up the next morning feeling better than she had felt since she was knocked out in the first round. She was good to go, and she decided to include breakfast out on her agenda. She had grown fond of Pancake Pantry and planned to enjoy her time there as if she didn't have a care in the world, which seemed like a normal plan for a woman who had recently suffered a concussion.

She left the chalet early and drove into the small town nestled in the valley below the mountains. As she drove into town she wondered again what it would be like to live in a town where first-time visitors are constantly bringing their smiling faces there to enjoy their vacation. And others are returning each year or two to recapture the magic they found there. She wondered what it would be like to own a small shop in the Village Shops, seeing new people each day, and seeing many of them return the next year to purchase something else.

She loved the stream that the locals called the Little Pigeon River, so her first choice was to see if she could find a parking place on River Road. Luck was with her, although she had to drive a few blocks to find an unoccupied spot. She got out of her car and pirouetted to see if she saw someone who wanted to make sure that she didn't have a nice day. Satisfied that no unscrupulous savages were around, she began to walk. Like before, she looked over the railing and down upon the Little Pigeon River. As she walked from her car to the restaurant, she continued to check to see if anyone seemed interested in her, particularly anyone who looked familiar to her.

She arrived at the restaurant without seeing a familiar face, or anyone who seemed to be more interested in her than they should be. She entered the restaurant, was seated, and studied the menu. She was determined to enjoy her day. A couple of minutes later, she placed her order and waited for it to arrive. She chose crepes filled with berries and cream cheese, and an order of bacon, with some orange juice, coffee, and water with lemon to wash it down. She was able to eat all of that without her husband, the stranger, or Carla joining her for breakfast. She was seated near the front, facing the large window, and the street. She looked at those passing by and occasionally took in the scenic mountain in the distance. When she hadn't recognized anyone by the time she got up to leave she continued with her plan to act like a tourist.

Pam was on her way to her vehicle when she heard her phone ring. She had programmed each of her ring tones differently, so she knew who was calling. She smiled as she reached for her phone.

"Hey, Mom! I was just getting ready to call you."

"Didn't anyone ever tell you that it's not a good idea to lie to your mother?"

"Okay. Here's the real spiel. I just finished breakfast, had some very good crepes, bacon, etc. As soon as I get back to my car I'm going shopping. Anything you want?"

"I could use some milk and bread. Listen, honey, I know you're on vacation, but after what that private investigator told me, I'm worried about you. I thought maybe that husband of yours had done away with you."

"He tried a couple of times, but the bullet just barely grazed my ear. The doctor said it might not even leave a scar, and it hasn't affected my hearing. After that happened, I removed all the bullets from his gun and took all sharp instruments away from him. I even took his belt and shoelaces."

"Could you just give me the truth?"

"Okay, but you're not going to like it. After I talked to that detective you hired, I got worried. I knocked Jack out, tied him up, and left him in a remote cabin where no one would find him until I could decide whether or not to go back and let him go. The only trouble is that I received a note telling me that someone had kidnapped Jack. Curious, I drove back there, was hit over the head with something, was tied up like Jack was, and was left there to die. But sometime later a handsome stranger came along and rescued me. Am I boring you so far?"

"No, just divorce Jack and bring the stranger back with you. Bring him over to dinner sometime. I'll invite the private detective over too, only we won't tell your stranger that my guy is a detective. Then I'll have the detective check him out, and if he doesn't appear to be the type who will murder you, you can marry him, whether he has money or not."

"What if I decide to take your detective and leave you with my vagrant?"

"Well, at least my guy will be handsome. That detective is as ugly as they come."

"Good. Then some other woman won't take him away from me."

"Just watch yourself. I don't do funerals well, and I never know what kind of flowers to send."

"Oh, that's okay. Just tell the florist you need a casket spray. You can even have them put on it, 'You Should Have Listened To Me, Love, Mom.' Listen, I'm back at my car now, and I want to get some shopping done before the sun goes down. Love ya, Ma!"

"Love you, too! I just wish you hadn't turned out like your dad."

"That reminds me, isn't he coming up for parole soon?"

"Not funny. But I'll tell him you said so when I go visit him at the cemetery on Friday."

+++

Pam ended her call and smiled. She and her mother had always been close, even though she didn't always follow the directions her mother gave her. Maybe she should have taken her mother's advice and beat it out of Dodge. But then, maybe Jack or someone he had hired would have killed her before she got away.

Since Pam didn't find a parking space until she was well down River Road, she continued on that road until she got to the high end of the Parkway. There she turned left and joined the other lemmings on the Parkway. Or were they processionary caterpillars? It didn't matter. She had a mind of her own, and her mind told her she needed to turn right at Traffic Light 3 and go up the hill to get to the Craft Loop. With the lights being marked by number and the numbers being consecutive, she had no problem knowing at what point she was to turn right. It was a little harder looking for Glades Road, where she was to turn left.

Nothing is ever the way we envision it, and that's the way it was with the Craft Loop. Pam pictured them to be a series of shops, just like the Village shops in Gatlinburg, side by side in an oval reminiscent of a large light bulb. As it turned out, it would have been a really big light bulb, because the craft loop covered eight miles of this and that. Instead of everything being right next to everything else, there were buildings of shops, then she had to drive to the next group of shops, with open spaces and trees in between. If she were to see all of the shops, which she knew she wouldn't have time to do, she would do almost as much driving as shopping. But what the Craft Loop offered that downtown Gatlinburg didn't was ample free parking at each group of shops. No paying five or ten dollars each time she got out of her vehicle.

Pam had found a full-color pamphlet with a thorough description of all the shops, so she identified the first place she planned to stop, pulled in and got out of her car. Like many things in the area, there were steps to climb to get to where she was going, but that was no problem for a woman her age, who was in good health.

The shops sold everything imaginable, with most of them specializing in one type of merchandise. Candles, candy, jewelry, pottery, woodworking, artwork, and fine quality merchandise at that. And over one hundred shops to choose from. Some of the shops contained merchandise made by the person looking her in the eye, not a small child in some poor Asian country. What many of the stores sold can't be found in big box stores.

Most of the shops in the first group interested Pam, so she took a while and looked through each one. As she exited a shop on the second level, she looked down upon the parking lot and jumped. There, seated on the passenger's side of a vehicle was the man she had seen at Pancake Pantry on her first visit. Not the one she told her mother was the handsome stranger, but the one she described as a criminal type. He wasn't looking in her direction, but she stepped back anyway, to hide herself the best she could, while still studied him to see what he was up to. He didn't appear to be up to anything. He didn't appear to be nervous about anything or anxious for his companion to return. He merely sat there doing nothing. Pam was about to give up on him, and head off to another shop when her phone alerted her that she had an incoming text.

THERE ARE SO MANY SHOPS TO CHOOSE FROM, AND SO LITTLE TIME LEFT TO DO SO. DON'T YOU THINK?

A Smoky Mountain Mystery

Pam looked around, checking to see if she spotted a familiar face. There were a couple of older men seated on a bench waiting for their wives and a family with two small children, but there was no one else. Who had sent the text, and where was he, or she? It couldn't have been the criminal type in the car. She was watching him the whole time. His hands were visible. He wasn't on a phone. But was the person who sent the text his partner? Were the two of them the ones who tied her up? Did they kidnap or murder Jack? She waited a couple more minutes, studying the man, but then she noticed that the two elderly men were looking at her and whispering to each other. It was time for her to look at some more shops. She saw this cute little shop that sold jewelry. She would be safe there. She wouldn't look out of place, and she didn't expect any man, old or dangerous, to come in and abduct her or whisper about why she was there.

Pam didn't stay in the jewelry shop long. She knew she must have looked nervous to the two clerks, because they kept glancing at her, then made eye contact with each other. She was sure they thought she was a shoplifter. She walked out. The two men's wives had just returned and were showing their unappreciative husbands what they had purchased. Pam walked by them and once again looked down at the parking lot. The car was still there, but the man was no longer in it. She left the level she was on and spotted another store that sold one of her weaknesses. It was a candy store. She opened the door and stepped inside. There was no one in there except the clerk, who smiled at her. She had forgotten about the man she was sure wanted to harm her until she heard a bell that signaled that someone else was entering the shop. She looked up and was relieved to find out it was the family with two small children. She could tell by the look on the children's faces that this was their favorite shop so far. Quickly, they

159

began to give their parents a list of candy they saw that they wanted. Pam selected a couple of items, paid for them, and walked out. Her head rotated as she stepped out the door, but she saw nothing out of the way. She scanned the area for the man. Not only was he gone, but the car was gone from the parking lot. Soon, she would be, too.

Pam didn't let spotting the stranger ruin her day. She shopped and parked, shopped some more and parked again, went from store to store, passing up the ones that didn't interest her. She did this without seeing the man again. After enjoying herself for three hours and making a few purchases, Pam got hungry. She consulted her map and saw that just around the bend was an English pub called The Fox and Parrot. Pam had had her share of Italian, Mexican, and Asian food over much of her thirty-plus years on the earth, but she didn't remember ever eating English pub food. It wasn't as if she had a bucket list, but if so she would have checked one more thing off her list that day.

Like everything before it, the pub wasn't as she envisioned. She pulled in the driveway and parked up against a tree. The place didn't look impressive. And when she climbed one set of steps of that old building, there was a sign telling her she needed to climb another. Once there, she opened the door, found that there were a few other customers in the pub at a time that was a little after the normal time to eat lunch. In seconds she was seated at a table. She looked over the restaurant. There were a few men at the bar, but no one she recognized. From the looks of them, they had the look of vacationers having a good time, not locals who hung out there every day and downed a few. These men ate as much as they drank, and she could tell from their conversation that not all of them were together. Still, they talked to the other men they met. People have a way of talking more to strangers on vacations than they do at home. When someone sees someone in the mall at home who is wearing a shirt or cap of their favorite team, they take it in stride. But if they see someone sporting a similar item when they are on vacation, they go up to them and strike up a conversation like they had just seen an old friend for the first time in a while.

A couple of the other tables were filled with people, who looked just like anyone else in a restaurant. The lone waitress approached her and took her order. She was torn between two dishes she had heard of, shepherd's pie and bangers and mash. She chose the first, and the bar-maid/waitress left. With nothing else to do, Pam continued to study the other patrons and the pub's decorations. She smiled at one sign which warned the customers not to be in any hurry to get their food. But her food did come; it tasted fine, and she ate and paid her bill and left.

Pam continued to check out the shops on her way back toward town, and since it was a loop, she returned to Traffic Light 3, and a look at the clock on the dash told her it was 5:13.

She had no husband to return to. She wasn't in a mood to cook, so she turned left and checked out the upper part of the Parkway, then searched until she found a restaurant that had been recommended to her, The Peddler Steakhouse. The restaurant was pricy, but the food made it worth it. Pam started with baked brie, baked with toasted almonds, and served with almond slices and bread, and found this dish a wonderful way to begin her dining experience. The mountain trout was divine, and the salad bar a worthy accompaniment, and she was fortunate enough to get a table by the window, looking out at the Little Pigeon River, her new favorite body of water. Pam could see why The Peddler was one of the most recommended places to eat in Gatlinburg.

+++

It was 7:32 when Pam pulled up in front of her chalet. She looked around, saw no one suspicious, then unlocked the car door and got out. Again, she looked around. She had abandoned her Vacationer mode and returned to her Frightened Woman mode. Well, at least a careful woman who didn't want to be bashed over the head again. Or worse.

28

Slowly Pam walked over to the front door and punched in the security code. She opened the door and pushed it back far enough to make sure that no one was hiding behind it. As if that would make a difference. Unlike at the dilapidated cabin, nothing came charging at her head to knock her unconscious. Unless what Pam learned in her self defense class helped her to defeat an attacker, she didn't figure she stood a chance of avoiding capture, especially if her assailant had a gun.

Seeing no one, and tired from her day of shopping and eating, Pam walked through to the back of the chalet and headed out the door to the hot tub. She walked out and turned it on, then walked back inside to wait for it to heat. Then she shed her clothes, walked out onto the deck and over to the hot tub and eased down into the water to soak away all her aches and pains from the day. She lay there, looking out upon a small part of God's beautiful creation and enjoyed the quiet. A few minutes later, just before the sun was about to duck below the mountains for the day, feeling much better, she arose from the water, dried off, and walked back into the house. It was then that she saw it and screamed.

Jack's gun was lying there on the coffee table. She could tell without picking it up that someone had fixed it to where it wouldn't fire again.

The contented woman who had just emerged from
the hot tub suddenly turned angry and afraid. She walked
over and picked up a bar stool, held it in front of her, ready
to wield it at the first person she saw.

"Where are you?"

When she received no answer to her question, she
asked another.

"Who are you?"

Again no one answered.

"Jack!"

She listened for the slightest noise but heard nothing. She thought of escaping, grabbing her clothes, driving
a short distance, and then if no one was following her, she
would pull over and get dressed. But the chalet was located
in a remote area. Wasn't it just as likely that whoever put
the gun on the table could just as easily be outside the door
waiting for her as inside the chalet? From her vantage
point, she could see all of the living room and kitchen area.
There was no one in either place. So, if someone was hiding
they would either have to be in one of the bedrooms or the
game room downstairs. The master bedroom was also on
the first floor. She decided to look there first. She eased
over, clutching the bar stool in front of her, holding it so
she was ready to strike if she encountered someone. She
had lifted it so that at the first movement of someone in
front of her she could send it crashing down upon his head.
Pity any mouse that scurried across the floor at that point.
A bar stool could do more damage than a mousetrap. But
then there are no degrees of dead. Dead is dead, as in what
Pam didn't want to be. A mouse didn't care how it looked
dead. Mice didn't offer a choice of an open or closed casket.

Pam shook her head rapidly back and forth to elimi-
nate her strange thoughts about mice. She needed to concentrate on the matter at hand. She had left the bedroom
door open, and no one had closed it. As she turned the corner and looked into the room, she saw nothing out of place.

164

No grinning man holding a gun, waiting for her. All that was left to check in the room was the closet. She had to set down the stool to open the closet door, but she picked it up again as the door was opening. No bodies hung in the closet, nor did any tumble out at her. No breathing person lurked in there waiting for her, either.

She checked off the first floor, headed to the second, barstool in hand, awkward as it was. It took only a couple of minutes of checking out that floor to realize that if anyone was inside the chalet, he was on the lower level. So, she headed down the steps to the game room, the barstool leading the way. There were no closet doors to check, and no one hiding under the pool table. Whoever had left the gun for her meant merely to frighten her. And whoever did it had succeeded.

After receiving no texts telling her she should put some clothes on, Pam took a couple of deep breaths, then climbed the steps back to the main floor. She had barely gotten there when someone knocked on her door. She hurried to the door, ready to bash someone with the barstool. She saw it was the stranger, started to open the door, then realized that she had neglected to get dressed. She managed to close the door without him seeing her, then opened it an inch or two.

"Sorry, I need to get dressed. Be right back."

Pam hurried over and slipped into her clothes. Then she rushed back to the door, opened it, and rushed back to the barstool in case he attacked her. She couldn't understand why she had conflicting opinions of the stranger. After all, he had been recommended by her mother sight unseen.

Pam smiled.

"What's so funny?"

"Oh, nothing. I told my mother about you. She told me to bring you home, so she could check you out."

"So, is your mother interested in me, or did the two of you forget you have a husband? At least you say you have a husband. So far all I know about you is that you're secretive, claim to have a husband, and have a habit of opening your door without getting dressed."

Pam wasn't sure whether she blushed or not.

"Sorry. I just haven't been myself lately."

"Don't change back. I'm finding the new you quite entertaining."

Pam turned serious.

"So, why are you here? You have a habit of showing up every time something happens."

"Oh, what happened this time? It doesn't look like someone tied you up."

"Oh, nothing. But I do want to know why you keep showing up."

"I just came by to check and make sure you're okay."

"So, you just happened to come by. Have you by any chance been here earlier today?"

" I have."

"And did you come in?"

"Sorry, I don't have the combination."

"So, you didn't leave me anything?"

"Why? Is it your birthday?"

"No. Never mind. So, why do you feel the need to check on me?"

"Because I can tell there's more to your situation than you're telling. I don't know why, but for some reason, I feel responsible for you."

"I bet you tell that to all the ladies."

"Well, I think it's better than, 'Do you come here often?' Don't you?"

"You still haven't told me who you are."

"And you still haven't told me why you're not yourself lately."

"And why should I tell you? Are you my keeper?"

"I just don't like to see people get hurt. Someone has already made you a prisoner once. They could try again. Or try something worse. I don't like seeing pretty ladies in danger."

"I appreciate your concern, but it's just that you always show up at the most opportune times."

"It must be the Boy Scout in me."

"And here I thought it was the training you received for your paper route."

"In other words, you don't think it has anything to do with me being a photographer."

"You haven't by any chance been hanging out in the trees taking pictures of me in the hot tub, have you?"

"No. I have a fear of heights."

"Just make sure you keep it. Well, I'm fine. I've already eaten, so you don't have to fix my dinner. And it's getting late. It's time for you to move on."

"It touches my heart to see that you're grateful for all that I've done for you."

"Okay. I'm grateful. I just wish you'd wait until I call and ask you for help."

"Sometimes waiting for a call means you get there too late. I don't want to know what the coroner feels like."

"Then stay away from him. I promise to lock the door and sleep with one eye open. Is that good enough for you?"

"No, but you're a grown woman. I just hope nothing happens to you."

+++

Pam watched the stranger take his hint and leave. She even heard him drive off. She wasn't sure if that was good or bad. What worried her the most was that he always showed up just after someone had done something terrible to her. That seemed like too much of a coincidence. So, who was this guy?

167

She knew that not everything is black or white. Some things are gray. But the one thing she knew was that the stranger wasn't gray. He was either the person who was terrorizing her, or he was the knight in shining armor, that she didn't need. Well, maybe as a rescuer, but nothing more. Somewhere she had a husband. At least she would have one until someone reports him dead, or someone is successful in ending her life.

29

The night was in full bloom. Pam knew her chances of survival were much greater inside the chalet than outside in the dark. While the chalet had three levels, unless someone was a mountain climber there were only two ways he could get inside; the front door that had a security code, and a sliding glass door on the lower level, that worked with a key.

Pam approached the stairs and turned on the light, then headed down, slowly, one step at a time. She turned another light on once she got to the switch. The drapes were pulled across the sliding glass door and all the windows, so Pam had no idea if someone was parked on the other side, ready to jump her if she came to the door. She grabbed a cue stick from the pool table and headed to the door. She looked around the drapes and peeked out. She couldn't see a thing. So, she turned on the outside light and looked quickly before a Peeping Tom could leave. No one was lurking outside the door. There were no bears a few feet from the house. She tried the door. It was unlocked. She locked the door and fumbled for the bar that prevented anyone from opening it. She dropped it into place on the track. Now, the only way anyone could get inside would be to break a window or use the code.

How long had the door been unlocked? Had it been unlocked the whole time they were there? She tried to recall if she had gone out that door. No. She had been outside the one on the main level many times. Outside the one on the upper level a few times. But hadn't gone out on the ground level in the back. Could it be that whoever entered the house came in through the sliding glass door rather than the front door? If so, that meant that it could have been anyone. Otherwise, it would have had to have been Jack, or the stranger who wanted to help her, who might have been looking over her shoulder when she punched in the code that day. Or did someone else have the code? Is it possible that this whole vacation had been Jack's plan to get rid of her, either by killing her or by disappearing and driving her crazy by attacking and tormenting her? While the vacation was her idea, Jack chose the location. And what better place to murder someone than an out-of-the-way chalet in the mountains. The look of the place would disarm anyone's negative thoughts. No one would expect to be murdered in a beautiful home with a fantastic view of the mountains. As was usually the case, Pam had more questions than answers. And she wasn't going to come up with any of those answers standing there. She pulled the drapes back over the door, regained her privacy, and trotted off up the steps to the main floor.

More and more it felt like the best thing to do would be to call the police, but Pam felt she still couldn't do that. She was afraid of being arrested. If it meant she had to fight, then she had to fight using whatever method she had available.

Pam tried to make herself feel better by telling herself that both times someone had come calling, they had done so in the daytime. That didn't mean she was safe in the chalet alone at night. But she made a decision. She would stay there that night, then sometime the next day she would try to locate a gun. Was there anywhere she could purchase one without a waiting period? Of course, there was. And if whoever it came back, Pam could surprise them and gain the upper hand. Then it was just a matter of whether she wanted to shoot them, or knock them out and throw the body down the mountain. Thoughts like that weren't normal for her. It was just that someone had messed with her, and Pam didn't like to be messed with. She didn't plan to succumb to their wishes. She planned to fight.

30

The Eleventh Day

Pam didn't want to be predictable, so the next morning when she woke up, she continued to lie in bed. Eventually, she got up and headed to the kitchen to fix herself some breakfast. She never learned to make sausage gravy, so she opted for bacon, eggs, and toast. She located two new jars of jam left by the owner for her to use. She wasn't going to leave it for the next person to rent the property. She was sure the owner would replenish the stock.

After eating and getting on the Internet for a few minutes, she picked up a cue stick for protection and headed out the door for a walk. It wasn't so much that she loved to exercise, which she could take or leave, but she wanted to scout out the immediate area just in case she had to beat a hasty retreat one day. She was surprised when she opened the front door and the stranger's car wasn't parked behind hers. There was no one else around, either. Nothing except some fragrant mountain air and a small part of the beautiful mountainside.

As she headed down the road in the direction to which she had never been, her agenda was fourfold. She wanted to see how many species of trees she could identify. She wanted to look for wildflowers. She hoped to see some non-threatening wildlife. And she hoped not to run into any other humans.

A half-mile later she had learned a couple of things. The road dead-ended, and there were no other dwellings on that road. No more than ten feet from the road she stood on the mountain declined steeply. The Smokies weren't foggy, so she was able to see over to the next mountain ridge. That ridge was of a similar height to the one on which she stood. On it too stood a chalet, but only one. She could see it from where she stood at that moment, a half-mile from the chalet where she was staying, but neither house could be seen from the other.

Pam looked hard at the chalet across the way. It looked even larger than hers, still with three levels, but more square footage on each level. She walked on a few feet, getting as close to the drop off as she could without endangering herself. She hoped to get an angle where she could see if there was anyone there. But she couldn't tell. What she could tell was that it would be extremely difficult for someone to get from that chalet to hers on foot, and the only way they could come to her place by car is the same way she had to get back each time she left.

She stood there a few minutes, then headed back to where she was staying. As she rounded the last turn she stopped, gasped, and backed up so she wouldn't be seen. Standing there near her chalet was the stranger she referred to as the one who looked like a criminal. And she could tell that he was carrying a gun. She was pretty sure that he hadn't seen her. At least he didn't take off running in her direction. And he was facing the other direction.

Pam backed up a little more, far enough around the curve to where she could cross the road and ease down the hill. It wasn't quite as steep there as it was on down, where she saw the other chalet.

She contemplated what to do. She thought she could ease back toward her chalet as long as she stayed ten feet or so below the road's surface. This worked for thirty or so feet, but then she had to dip even farther because the trees weren't as thick. But what if the stranger had seen her and was doing the same thing she was. She stopped for a minute. Listened. She heard nothing that signified that she wasn't the only person up on the mountain. But why was the man there? He wasn't hiding behind her SUV. He was out in the open. And he wasn't near the door of her chalet, so it wasn't as if he was planning to jump her when she walked out the door, just in case he hadn't seen her leave and figured she was inside.

Pam waited a couple more minutes, and then she began her trek again, only more slowly this time. Just as she did, it started pouring down rain. The trees deflected most of it, but she was still getting wet. She came to a place where the decline was steeper and slid downhill a couple of feet before she could grab a branch and steady herself. She remained there a couple of minutes, breathing a little heavier than normal. She didn't want to spend the rest of the morning there, getting soaked, so she moved on. She slipped back into a covering thick with trees, evergreens whose branches drooped to the ground. This was perfect for easing back up to the road and checking to see where the stranger was. It also protected her more from the rain. She crawled up the hill toward the road, slowly and quietly, so as not to be seen or heard. A couple of minutes later she found herself on relatively flat ground. She clutched a branch and pulled herself to her feet with one hand while she grasped the cue stick with the other. She stood there, as silently as possible, not daring to move too quickly. Then slowly she moved a branch just enough to where she could see. It was all she could do to keep from screaming. He wasn't more than twenty feet in front of her. Luckily she was quiet and he was facing the other direction, plus the rain prevented him from hearing what little sound she made. She eased the branch back in place and stood there, not wanting to make a noise and alert him that she was nearby. After five more minutes, the rain stopped. It had been a downpour, but one of short duration.

A couple of minutes later she heard a car approaching. She wanted to see who it was, but she was afraid to move. Whoever it was had to be this guy's partner or his adversary. Pam heard the car stop near where she was. Then she heard a door open and then close a few seconds later and then the car took off. It was a good thing that Pam had scouted out the road because otherwise she would have jumped out and started running to her chalet as soon as the car was out of sight. But the car took off toward the dead-end, so she knew that it would either park there or turn around and head back in her direction. And that's exactly what they did. Pam was afraid to move the branch until the car had passed her, but then she chanced it and looked at the car moving down the road at a normal rate of speed. But the car was far enough away from her that she couldn't identify what kind of car it was, let alone the driver. It could have been a man or a woman. She couldn't even tell that. This time as soon as the car was out of sight, she waited a couple of seconds and then took off running to safety. It wasn't far, and she was in good physical condition, so she was able to get to the house, punch in the code, and get inside the house undetected. She stood near the door for a couple of minutes, listening to find out if the car returned, but she heard nothing.

It took Pam only a couple of minutes to calm down, to feel safe again inside the chalet. But she didn't plan to spend the day there. She pulled out her phone. 10:47. She had plans unless she opened the door to leave and found out she had company. She hurried to the shower. Ten minutes later, after washing off the dirt and sweat from her morning escapade and washing her hair, she jumped out of the shower and headed to the bedroom to get dressed. She planned to drive to Pigeon Forge for lunch, and later to buy a gun. She had found a place online, where she could buy a gun at a show going on in Pigeon Forge. She would have to register the gun, but she would acquire her protection that day, and that was what she wanted. She didn't care if every policeman in the United States knew she was carrying. She just wanted to feel safe again.

31

When Pam pulled into the parking lot at Mel's Diner, she gazed upon a facade that was like nothing she had seen growing up. The diner looked much like a long white trailer with large windows. For a moment she felt she had stepped onto the set for the *Happy Days* TV show. Once inside the diner, she found it to be a young person's paradise. The fare included hamburgers, hot dogs, and banana splits. And of course, there was a jukebox.

She took her time eating lunch, and when she left, she headed straight for the show where she could find someone who could sell her a gun. She had no particular make or model in mind. She would let the seller advise her, and since there were several dealers selling guns there, if one didn't seem to have her best interest in mind she would walk over to another one. She didn't need a gun that would blow a hole in someone at two hundred yards. She merely wanted something she could handle that would discourage the riffraff from messing with her. The problem was that she didn't know who the riffraff was. After looking around for a few minutes, talking to a few dealers, and handling some guns to see how each of them felt, she bought the gun that she felt was best for her.

Other than when she and Jack had driven through Pigeon Forge on their way to the cabin, and when they saw the Hatfield's & McCoy show that night, Pam had spent all of her time in Gatlinburg. It was closer to where she was staying. Because she had forgotten what she had seen as she and Jack drove through Pigeon Forge, after she secured the gun, she checked out the small town.

The only similarity between Pigeon Forge and Gatlinburg is that both of them are small, touristy towns located a few miles apart. Gatlinburg is a small town more nestled in the mountains, with shops right on the street, and parking at a distance. Pigeon Forge has a much wider road, with more lanes, bigger stores and larger attractions, and parking between the street and those stores and attractions.

It sounds like it's easy to find a parking place, and sometimes it is, but it's harder to find parking at some stores than others. One of those is a store called The Incredible Christmas Place, a store that keeps on going and going and going. That store would be a vacation destination itself for someone who has a Christmas tree in every room. And if a family had room for a Christmas tree in every room, but had only one tree, this store has enough different trees that a person could buy all the trees they want and the store would ship them home for them. It's a store where a shopper can easily get lost inside.

The Incredible Christmas Place was Pam's next destination. Once she found a parking space off to the side near the rear of the store, she walked to the front and entered one of many doors that allowed her inside. Stunned by the enormous size of the store, which looked much larger on the inside than it did from the parking lot, she began to shop. It was in her second of the store's many rooms that she looked up and saw a familiar face. Carla must have sensed this because she looked up right after Pam saw her.

"Are you still following me?"

"I see that you and Jack haven't made up."

"How do you know that? Jack's never been one for shopping. So, what brings you here, or are you still following me?"

"I'm doing a little shopping, even considering buying a new tree for Christmas. The one I have now is twelve years old."

"You know how old your tree is?"

"I do, but only because I remember the year I got it. It was my mother's last Christmas. But enough about that. Now, I know why you're here."

Pam gave Carla a quizzical look, but Carla just nodded her head. Pam turned and her shoulders slumped.

"What are you doing here?"

"Well! Well! Well! What brings you here, Mrs. Archer?"

"You can cut out the Mrs. Archer routine. I know the two of you are lovers."

"Who is this misguided individual?"

"This is Carla, my husband's secretary."

"Today people refer to us as administrative assistants."

"This is my husband's administrative assistant, and she may be even more than that to him."

"Don't go accusing me to get yourself off the hook. I know the two of you have been seeing each other."

"What's she talking about?"

"She saw both of us at Pancake Pantry one morning, the day I stopped by your table, and she thinks you and I have something going on. She might even think we've done something with my husband."

"Really?"

"Really. He does seem to have disappeared, and Mrs. Archer doesn't seem to care where Mr. Archer is."

"That's not true. By the way, have you seen your other boss down here?"

"Bernie?"

"That's the only other boss I know you have."

"Is he here, too?"

"That's what I'd like to know."

"Me, too. Maybe I should hang out with you ladies more often."

"Who is this guy?"

"I don't know. He hasn't introduced himself yet, but he keeps showing up at the most inconvenient times."

"And now I'll disappear. Good luck with your shopping, ladies."

Pam spent a couple more minutes talking to Carla and then spent over an hour of her afternoon checking out the store that sold all the Christmas decorations known to mankind. It was a long way until Christmas, and Pam wasn't sure what her next Christmas would be like, or if she would be around at Christmas. But most people feel better when they think of Christmas, and the time she spent in the Christmas store, and the friendly greetings she received from the employees in each area of the store, put a smile on her face. Before she left, she noticed Carla cart out a couple of large bags, and an employee carting a large box out to Carla's car. It was large enough to hold a Christmas tree.

With more time ahead of her and the fact that she had conserved energy by not having to dodge bullets, she drove to the far side of Pigeon Forge and took in the exhibit that gave her a little idea of what it felt like to be on the Titanic. She was given a boarding pass when she entered. This pass had the name of one of the Titanic's passengers. She was told she would learn the fate of that passenger before she left. An hour and a half later, she learned that the passenger whose name she held had survived to enjoy America. She was hoping that was a good sign for her.

When she left the Titanic replica a little after 5:00, she learned that not all the traffic in the area was in Gatlinburg. She had seen some traffic earlier, but, like everywhere else, 5:00 traffic in Pigeon Forge was heavier than earlier in the day. She wondered if people live in this vacationland, and if they do, do they get off work at 5:00 the way normal people in normal places do? The road was wider. The traffic was heavier. And Pam found a way to get out of that traffic, at least for a while. She spotted Mellow Mushroom Pizza off to her left. She knew their pizza was good. She had eaten at the one in Lexington. She found a place to park and soon learned that this Mellow Mushroom was larger than the one in Lexington. It was a good thing too because she wasn't the only one who wanted pizza that night.

Pam took her time eating, While she ate, she played a trivia game she saw on one of the many TVs in the restaurant. When she finished eating, she saw that the traffic had thinned somewhat, so she got up to return to the chalet. She turned left out of the parking lot and drove past all the signs advertising every area attraction crying for her money. As she left Pigeon Forge behind, she encountered a short scenic drive that reminded her how beautiful the area is. To help out-of-towners to better enjoy the drive, the road that meanders through the trees and past a section of the Little Pigeon River has a lower speed limit. Pam's turnoff to the cabin was not far past the Gatlinburg Visitor's Center. This allowed her to miss most of the traffic that was about to enter Gatlinburg. As she turned left and headed to her chalet, she thought of the hot tub that would soothe her muscle aches once she arrived.

Close to a half-hour later, she arrived and was relieved to find that there were no more guns and no people, alive or dead, to welcome her home. It had been a fun day. Well, as fun as a day can be when part of your agenda is to buy a gun so you can shoot someone before they shoot you.

+++

Pam had only the rest of that night, plus two more days and part of the next morning to enjoy the chalet and her vacation if you could call what she was doing enjoying it. She couldn't understand why, with all the money Jack had, they had never bought a hot tub for their home, but that would change, provided she found Jack, he didn't try to kill her, and they lived happily ever after. After she returned to the chalet, she spent a few minutes relaxing in the hot tub, and the rest of the night relaxing on the long parapet, deck, or whatever they called it. When the insects got too bad, she went inside.

32

The Twelfth Day

Pam put off planning the following day until she woke the next morning, and as it turned out, she didn't have to plan it after all. Well, at least the first part of the day. Pam awoke and made no effort to rise out of the bed. She lay there enjoying the king-size bed well into the morning until she heard a knock at the door. Startled by the fact that someone was knocking on her door, she contemplated whether or not to get up and answer it. Whoever it was had to be someone who knew she was inside, so she jumped up out of bed. She was fairly certain she knew who it was. It could only be the mysterious stranger. No one else had called on her. Well, except for that policeman who wasn't a policeman, and she figured that he wouldn't return. But she did wonder what had happened to him. She hadn't seen him since that morning when he called on her to see if her husband was still missing. She wasn't sure who the man was, or where he was because she hadn't seen him since. But she figured he called on her because he was either her husband's accomplice or working for someone else, like Bernie, who might be using the man to murder Jack.

Pam thought again about not answering the door, but she pulled on a robe, tied it around her, and hurried off to see who was there. She looked out and it was indeed who she thought it was.

"You again!"

"So nice to see you, too. No Pancake Pantry today?"

"I called and canceled my reservation. I didn't realize I needed to inform you, too."

"Anyway, these are for you," he said as he handed her a dozen donuts. "I'm afraid breakfast will be a little late this morning."

"Oh!" was all Pam could think of to say, and she turned away from the door and walked over to the kitchen table to set down the donuts. He followed her inside.

"Yeah. My vacation is over. I'm back at work now."

"You mean you're doing a photoshoot of my chalet or that I'm one of the customers on your paper route?"

"I see that you saw through my not-so-clever charade, which I didn't expect you to believe anyway. Neither, my dear lady. I'm Nick Hartsong. I'm a special agent with the FBI."

"They said you'd try that."

"They who? And try what?"

"They contacted me the other day and told me to beware of you, that you would get desperate and claim to be with the FBI."

"Let's try this again. Who contacted you, and how did they contact you?"

"I don't know who it was, but I received a note, but it wasn't like any of the other notes I received."

"And you are inclined to believe an anonymous note over my word. Okay. Here are my credentials. Look at them."

"They said those would look authentic, too."

"Listen, Mrs. Archer, I am a special agent with the FBI, and I'm now here on official business."

"How come you're always by yourself. Where are the others? Don't you usually work as a team?"

A Smoky Mountain Mystery

"When I saw you before I was on vacation. I wasn't working on any case. Just enjoying myself. Even though you looked suspicious I was determined to enjoy my vacation the best I could."

"Me? Look suspicious? You were the one following me. You were the suspicious one. I didn't do anything to involve you."

"Everything that you did, the way you looked shouted, 'This is not an ordinary woman on vacation.'"

"I had things on my mind."

"I could tell. And now I have things on my mind. I have some questions for you. What can you tell me about your husband?"

"That he's missing. You already know that."

"I mean before you came to Tennessee."

"Well, that he's my husband and a co-owner of a large successful business. Is that enough?"

"How long have you know him?"

"We've been married for six years. I met him a few months before we married. Why are you so concerned about my husband many years ago, and not so concerned that he seems to be missing as we speak? That is unless you know where he is."

"No, I'm sorry to say we don't have a clue where he is. And we don't have a clue who he is."

"What do you mean? He's Jack Archer, of Archer & Carlucci, a successful businessman, not only in Kentucky but around the world."

"That may be who he is now, but there's no record of anyone named Jack Archer before seven years ago. Oh, there are several Jack Archers. You can find some of them on Facebook. It's just that none of them are *your* Jack Archer. Not only that, but there's no record of a Bernie or Bernard Carlucci before seven years ago, either."

"I don't know about Bernie, but Jack lived somewhere else before we met. He wasn't from Kentucky."

"Mrs. Archer, the FBI has offices all over the country. A Jack Archer, at least a Jack Archer who could be your husband, hasn't been anywhere before seven years ago."

"Well, maybe he changed his name. Is that a crime?"

"No, but we're checking into whether or not he changed his name because he committed a crime. Who knows? He might be married to someone else, too. Maybe you and Mr. Archer aren't married."

"I don't think so unless his other wife lives in Lexington. He may come home late a lot, but he has always come home, so he hasn't had time to go visit another family in another state. And most men who have two families don't have both families in the same town. It's too easy to get caught."

"Well, he hasn't gotten caught before now. Maybe he had another wife and family and murdered them, left the area, and changed his name. Maybe that's where he got his money."

Pam shuddered at the agent's words.

"Well, it's obvious he didn't marry me for my money. I wasn't destitute, but I didn't have enough money that someone would marry me for it."

"Maybe he married you so he would fit in, figured the law enforcement from where he came from wouldn't be as suspicious of a married man."

"I just thought of something. I doubt if this has anything to do with Jack, but some guy called Jack and when I told him about it the name seemed to unnerve Jack."

"So who called him?"

"I don't know. But he said he was from the Berium Corporation and he wanted to get hold of Jack."

"The Berium Corporation?"

"That's right."

"Maybe you heard him wrong."

"No, I'm sure that's what he said."

"Haven't you heard of the Berium Corporation?"

186

"No. Should I have?"

"They were in the news a few years ago. Let me see. I think it was eight years ago. They were a large company and they found out two of their upper management employees had embezzled well over one million dollars from them."

"Well, this guy said the Berium Corporation. Maybe it's another company of the same name."

"But you say he didn't give you his name?"

"Well, he did say for Jack to get in touch with one of two guys. Let me see. I wrote their names down and put them in my purse. Just a second. Let me get my purse.

"Okay. Here it is. He said to call either Bob Cartwright or Vince Allred."

"That's the names of the two guys who embezzled all the money."

33

"So, why were these two guys calling Jack? Even if Jack knew them it would make more sense for them to avoid him."

"I agree. And I doubt if whoever called your husband was either of those two men unless your husband stole the money that they embezzled and they are just now able to find him. Which could make sense, since we're just now looking into his past. But let me back up and tell you what we know for sure. Cartwright and Allred's car plunged over a mountain pass and burned. We don't know if it happened the day they disappeared, but it wasn't found for several weeks. When they found it, it was wedged between a rock face and a large tree. This happened in such a remote area, that searching for them was hard, but a rescue party tried. Their bodies were never found, but the car was found hanging in mid-air, on its side, with one door open. The car was well below where it skidded off the road, but well above any land below. So, there's a possibility that whoever was inside, provided someone was inside when it left the road, fell out the door and down to who knows where."

"So you don't know if they were in the car when it went over, or if they staged the whole thing?"

"That's right. But if they did stage it, they were lucky. The car had burned. We have no idea if they escaped, or not."

"But then there's also the possibility that he could be alive and that one of those embezzlers was the name I now call my husband? So who is this guy who called Jack?"

"I have no idea. All I know is that the insurance company gave up on their investigation and settled a long time ago, so I doubt if whoever called you works for them. One possibility is that someone thinks your husband and his partner are the two embezzlers. Maybe this guy is a blackmailer. Or maybe one of the embezzlers got away with the money, and that person was the other guy wanting his half of the money. But my best guess is that I don't know who the guy who called you is, but maybe he thinks the two embezzlers are still alive and they're now going by the names of Jack Archer and Bernie Carlucci. This happened about a year before you met your husband. Did he have money when you married?"

"Well, we had enough to get married on, but not a lot. No. It was a couple of years later before Jack struck it rich."

"Or it could have been a couple of years later when Jack felt safe enough to start spending the money he stole? Do you have any idea where your husband might be at this moment?"

"None whatsoever."

"Okay. How about Bernie Carlucci? Any idea where he is?"

"Yeah, he's on vacation."

"Where?"

"I don't know where. See, I called the office the other day to check and see if Jack returned to Lexington, and to work. He hasn't been there since we left to come here. They told me that Bernie left to go on vacation right after Jack did. And their secretary, Carla Rogers, left to go on vacation, too. You know, the one I introduced you to yesterday, who thought you and I have something going on."

"We're not concerned with Miss Rogers. Nor Mrs. Carlucci. Nor you. All of you have used the same name for your entire lives, other than the fact that two of you changed your name when you got married. Now, think about this. This is a serious business. It could be that both your husband and Bernie Carlucci, or whoever they are, skipped town after the nosy guy showed up."

"Well, he didn't show up."

"But you don't know if he called from Lexington or somewhere else, do you?"

"No, but he didn't call until the day before we left on vacation, and our vacation had been planned for a few weeks before he called. It isn't as if Jack left town because he was scared."

"Maybe it happened at a convenient time. Had Carlucci planned to go on vacation, too?"

"I don't know. Remember, only the two of us knew that we were going on vacation."

"As far as you know, no one else knew. But here's what we know. We know your husband is missing, and now you have a third element to add to the equation. Your husband could be dead. He could be kidnapped and being held somewhere. Or he could have used this trip to escape from you and the demons of his past. If this is true, and he is one of these two men, he's done it before, so it would be no problem for him to do it again. Do I have your permission to check your bank account and see if there has been a large withdrawal lately?"

"Jack has money in several different accounts. I'll check the ones I know and let you know if a lot of money is missing."

"Can you do that today?"

"I'll do it as soon as you leave. Now in the meantime, do you mind if I call the FBI to see if they have an agent with your name?"

"They won't tell you. That information is confidential. You'll just have to trust me."

"I trusted the other cop who was here, but when I checked on him I found out that he's not a cop after all. He hasn't been back, so I'm not concerned about him. I just told you this because just because someone tells you he's law enforcement, it doesn't mean that he is."

"Well, usually he is, but I agree. There are exceptions. but you're going to have to cooperate."

"But I don't see how I can help you."

"I'm not sure you can, either. But do you have any idea at all who might have tied you up and left you in that cabin?"

"If I answer that question, do you promise you won't arrest me?"

"Are you saying that you had a friend tie you up because I know that you couldn't have done it yourself?"

"No. Someone did it, all right. I'm just not sure who it was."

"But there's something you're not telling me. I know there is. I'm good at what I do."

"Okay. I'll trust you. Not long after we got here I received a phone call when I was out by myself. The caller was a private detective my mother hired and he told me he thought my husband was planning to kill me. When I returned here, Jack told me he wanted me to go for a ride with him. Having just heard that he planned to kill me, I panicked. I convinced him to let me show him this cabin, and then I used ether to knock him out. I didn't know what to do after that, so I came up with the idea of tying up Jack and leaving him there while I decided what to do. See, I wasn't sure if Jack was planning to murder me or not."

"I don't know how securely you tied up your husband. Do you think there is any way he might have been able to escape from that cabin by himself?"

"I don't think so. I used duct tape, just like what was used on me. I taped him to two pipes over by the sink. I bound his wrists together and his feet together. He was secured pretty well, and I took his cell phone and knife, so I don't think there was any way he could have gotten loose by himself. But I don't think we were followed, either. At least I didn't see anyone."

"I think I can answer that question for you. Someone put a tracking device on the back of your car. I have no idea if that was done before you left home or after you arrived here. It could have even happened after you left your husband in that cabin. It doesn't matter when. But that device allowed someone to stay far enough back that you couldn't see them, but they were aware of where you were at all times, provided they were close enough to your car."

"So, they could have come and taken Jack away, and they could have come back and tied me up after they rigged that board to knock me out. And just so you know that my brain works too, I'd say that at some point you put one of those devices on my car, and that's how you found me that day, and keep showing up wherever I am since then."

The agent merely smiled.

"So who came back for Jack?"

"I can't tell you. I can't even tell you if it was friend or foe."

Pam thought about the gravity of that situation.

"So we don't know if Jack is off somewhere getting the last laugh, or if he has already breathed his last breath."

"I think you hit the nail on the head."

"Oh, there's one other thing. I didn't tell you this, but someone's been in this chalet when I wasn't here. Someone came in one day and left Jack's battered gun, the one I took from him, and they left it just to terrify me. I checked the place thoroughly when I returned, mad and scared, but they merely wanted me to know that they can get in."

"Does your husband know the security code here?"

"Yeah, he was the one who unlocked the door when we first arrived."

"So, whoever was here was either your husband or someone who used your husband's knowledge of the security code to get inside."

"Not necessarily. See, I went downstairs and found out that the door down there was unlocked. I don't know if it was unlocked when we arrived the first day, or if someone broke in and unlocked it when they left, so I won't know who I'm dealing with."

"Really! I'm surprised you're still here. Do you have a death wish?"

"No, but I want to put an end to this thing. And since then I bought and registered another gun to protect myself, and I do know how to use it."

"Just be careful. Whoever it is might be someone you trust."

"No, I don't think my mother would do it, and she's the only one I trust at the moment."

"So, you still don't trust me?"

"Let's say my trust of you keeps fluctuating back and forth."

"I just hope you start to trust me before someone kills you. Speaking of your mother, did you check with her to see if the guy she hired was a private detective?"

"He was. She hired him, and she thought he was a detective. That's all I can tell you."

"And all I can tell you is to be careful. Don't let anyone in here except for me, and if you see or hear anything suspicious give me a call. Here's my card. And please don't call me Brucie again."

"I never did. It doesn't fit you. So, does this mean that you'll be working in this area?"

"Because I was already somewhat familiar with the case, I got myself assigned to it. So I'll be here as long as the government can afford to keep me here. How much longer do you plan to stay?"

"We have this place rented through the end of the week. I'm supposed to leave Friday morning by 10:00. Somebody has rented it and can arrive anytime after 3:00 that day. When I leave here, I think I'll go home and wait and see what happens."

"Just remember to be careful, and call me if you need me. And don't do anything else stupid."

+++

Special Agent Nick Hartsong left. Pam wasn't sure whether to believe him or not. All she knew was that he had had many opportunities to harm her and he hadn't done so. On the other hand, nothing he had said or done made her think of him as an FBI agent, special, whatever that meant, or otherwise. So, in a way she was still in a quandary on whether or not to trust him. But he was handsome. She hoped he was who he said he was. Oh, she didn't care if he was an agent or not, but she hoped he wasn't a criminal.

34

As the stranger drove off, Pam let out a big breath. What would happen next? But her thoughts quickly shifted from what would happen next, to what might have already happened. Was it possible that Jack wasn't who he told her he was? Could it be that he never loved her, that he married merely for convenience, and to hide from anyone who might be seeking him? But then Pam wondered if she ever loved him. Did she love him? Or did she marry him simply because she wanted a husband? It wasn't the money. If Jack had any money in the beginning, she didn't know about it. The money had indeed kept her from leaving him later, but not for marrying him in the first place. Did she think that this vacation might save their marriage? She thought about that. Yes, it wasn't just a vacation that she sought. She wanted a better marriage and felt like a vacation might start things off on a new track. But what did Jack think? And was he behind his disappearance, or was someone else responsible?

After hearing what the man who was now calling himself Nick Hartsong had to say, Pam was afraid her husband might be this man, and that he had left her and raided the bank account. She hurried to her phone. She checked the two joint accounts. There were no significant withdrawals from either of them, but Pam knew that Jack had other accounts, too. At least if Jack was one of these two embezzlers and he had left her, he had not left her broke.

+++

It was almost 11:00 when Special Agent Hartsong left. By the time her thoughts returned to the moment at hand Pam was starved, too starved to drive somewhere, find a place to park, walk, order, and wait to be served. So she hurried to the refrigerator to see what she had to eat. Was there enough food there for her to eat if she didn't leave the chalet that day? She looked and there was.

As she took the bacon and eggs from the refrigerator and set them on the counter next to the stove, she looked down and saw the donuts Hartsong had left. She opened the box, took one out, and crammed it into her mouth. There was chocolate icing on the outside, and the custard on the inside oozed out as she took her second bite. She took her tongue, ran it across the custard. and licked her lips. Chocolate icing with custard filling was her favorite. How did Hartsong know? Surely, even if he was an FBI agent he wouldn't know her favorite kind of donut. Well, it wasn't a donut. It was an éclair. She polished off the first one and picked up another. This one cherry-filled, with cream cheese, another of her favorites. They certainly weren't day-old leftovers at a bargain price. If she saw him again she would have to find out where he did his shopping. She looked at the remaining pastries in the box. If she ate over three she would forget the bacon and eggs. But she knew that if she did that she would get a sugar high and then be starved again before long, so she closed the box and pulled the rest of what she needed for a late breakfast from the refrigerator. As the bacon fried and sizzled in the skillet, she checked to see what the refrigerator held for later in the day. There was enough to eat that she wouldn't have to have donuts and bacon for lunch and supper. The

196

filet she saw laying on the refrigerator shelf was destined to cook on the grill on the deck until it had reached a status of medium-well. There was even a baked potato in a wooden larder and salad fixings in the refrigerator.

What had begun as a foggy day in the mountains had turned into a sunny day. The nice weather inspired Pam to carry her breakfast plate and glass of orange juice out onto the deck. There was a table, large enough for four, but still an okay place to eat if three of the seats were empty. Even if dining alone bothered her, no one could see that she had to eat by herself. But then she had been doing that for days, and in places a lot more public than where she was. She sat there and ate as the breeze blew through her hair. As she sat, she thought. In two days she would be leaving the chalet and heading home. Until then, she planned to enjoy her two days as if she was a single woman on vacation, which was pretty much how she had enjoyed most of the first eleven days of her vacation. Well, those days out of the eleven that she could say she enjoyed.

She quickly decided that she would spend the rest of that day at the chalet, and spend her last full day of her Smoky Mountain vacation in Gatlinburg or Pigeon Forge, seeing some of the sights she had missed.

With no agenda and a beautiful view in front of her, she sat there enjoying the breeze long after she had finished eating her breakfast. Almost two weeks there, and nary a neighbor anywhere. She wouldn't want it that way for the rest of her life, but she liked it at that moment.

Finally, she got up, grabbed her dishes, walked inside and put them in the sink, then headed up to the top floor. Even from the top step, the view through the large glass window across the room was magnificent. The far wall was nothing but glass, with a door she could walk through and a wooden parapet that ran the width of the house. There were bedrooms on each end of the house, but she walked straight ahead. She slipped off her robe, let it fall to the floor, and walked outside to the view that looked like she was on the top of the world. She rested her arms on the railing and looked out as if she was looking down on her kingdom. She stood there, confident in who she was. At least for that moment, she wasn't a woman afraid. She wasn't a woman mad at whoever was trying to ruin her life. Whoever it was, she wouldn't let him.

As she stood there, she had no idea how far she could see, but she knew it was farther than she imagined. Maybe that was North Carolina in the distance, rather than just outside Gatlinburg. Was that ridge in the distance part of the Great Smoky Mountain National Park where she and Jack had spent a day, where one of the strangers she saw at Pancake Pantry on the first day had chosen the same place on the same day? She doubted it. But it was still beautiful. She felt like singing *On A Clear Day You Can See Forever*. She pictured what the view would look like in the fall when the leaves burst into many different brilliant colors, and again what it would look like after a major snowstorm. Even if Jack was out of her life and no one else was to enter it, she still might come back to this same chalet to see what indeed it looked like in the fall and the winter.

She soaked in the beautiful view and made a mental note to come back that evening, just before sunset. Maybe that would be where she would eat her steak, baked potato, and salad. Or maybe she would get up in time to enjoy the next day's sunrise there, armed with the rest of the éclairs.

Time went by so slowly, and she didn't mind a bit. It wasn't like she had a job. It wasn't like she had an agenda, somewhere to be at a certain time. Pam went from one kind of soaking to another. She walked down one level and out onto the deck. She lifted the top off the hot tub, and let it warm up. Then she slid down into the water and wished she had two more weeks to enjoy her paradise.

Paradise. Was it a paradise without Jack? Was it even more of one because he wasn't there? She hoped not.

She wondered how different her life would be when she returned home if Jack was to never be a part of her life again. If he had run away, would he clean out the bank accounts? If so, would it matter to her? She felt if she was honest with herself, she would want to be comfortable, but she could live and be happy without being rich.

Before she turned into a prune, Pam rose out of the water, stepped out of the hot tub, and dripped a trail of water until she came to the towel she had left in a chair nearby. She dried herself, then slipped back into the robe she had carried down from upstairs.

She lingered on the deck a few minutes, then walked inside and took a shower. but her day was far from over. Before it ended, she would check out the lower level of the chalet, shoot pool and throw darts. She spent a little time on the computer seeing what life was like for those who weren't quite as fortunate as she was. And she did enjoy that sunset with her dinner. Only when the insects became too much for her did she head back inside and begin to plan her last full day in the mountains. And as she did, she helped herself to one more of the éclairs that Hartsong had brought. It was sticky, with cinnamon, a maple flavor, and pecans.

35

The Thirteenth Day

Pam went to bed a little earlier that night because she planned to get up and get started early the next morning. She set her alarm for just before daylight, fixed herself a cup of coffee, and mounted the steps to the third level. Sunrises make a person feel better no matter where they are and seem to add an extra oomph when someone is on vacation. But there is one big difference between sunrise in the mountains and one at home. In the mountains, the sun rises later and sets earlier than it does if you live in a flat area. But when the sun comes up over the mountain, it is a beautiful sight and each morning when Pam woke up she couldn't get enough of it. And that was true of the thirteenth day of her vacation, too. The sunrise didn't disappoint her. It was magnificent, even though her view from the back window and the balcony didn't face directly east, and the sun had to rise above the mountain before she could get the full effect of a mountaintop sunrise.

She lingered only a few minutes after daylight because she had planned to pack as much into her day as she could, then come back a little before dark and soak away her aches and pains in the hot tub.

She drove down the mountain without encountering another car until she got to the East Parkway. She arrived in town before most everyone else was out and about. She had breakfast at her usual place and managed to secure a table right beside the front window. A scrumptious breakfast and a breathtaking view. What more could she want? Well, maybe a loving husband who was beside her and no one around who wished her harm.

Pam didn't bother to look and see if any of the usual suspects were dining with her. She finished her breakfast and walked down to River Road. It was a few minutes before the attractions she was interested in opened, but she had the Little Pigeon River all to herself. Well, at least a small portion of the river. She had already taken photographs of the picturesque scene, so she didn't bother to pull out her camera. Instead, she looked up, down, and around, and saw Gatlinburg at its most peaceful time. Well, at one of them.

By the time 12:30 had rolled around, Pam had been to Christ in the Smokies, a wax museum where the figures represented different people and moments in the Bible, and visited the Ripley's Aquarium of the Smokies, which produced a different smell than anywhere else she had been. While at the aquarium, she lingered the longest as she watched the penguins. Each time she had gone to a zoo, she was amazed at how small penguins are and how large a moose is. Before that, her knowledge of penguins and moose were the cartoon characters Chilly Willy and Bullwinkle.

She walked out of the aquarium and instantly the smells of the nearby Mexican restaurant, No Way Jose, wafted through the air. She had overheard someone say how good the food there was and how reasonably priced it was. She only had to wait for a table a couple of minutes and was seated at a corner table where she perused the menu. Forty-five minutes later, she finished her meal and ate the most wonderful dessert she had ever had in a

Mexican restaurant. She agreed with the others. The food was good and inexpensive.

As she ate, she thought about what was ahead of her. She knew she wasn't in any hurry to get home the next day, and had no reason to go back. She had to be out of the chalet by 10:00, but she would play it by ear as to what time she would leave the area. If she got away in time to get home before dark, she would go all the way home, but if not, she would stop somewhere and drive the rest of the way the next day. It was nice to have enough money that it didn't limit her plans, and to have no agenda to get back to, so she could come and go as she pleased. Only the fact that the chalet was rented to someone else for the next several days meant she would have to leave it behind. So, she decided to put off her shopping until her last day in Gatlinburg before she left town.

Considering what she had to endure and figuring that her husband no longer loved her, she had enjoyed most of her vacation. But in a way, it would be good to get back home. Would she be going back to a completely different life? She had no idea, and no idea when she would find out. She merely knew that there was someone who said he was an FBI agent who was looking for her husband, and she would leave that job to him. Besides, she still didn't know if Jack was alive, and if so, if Jack was wishing her dead. She merely knew that there was a private detective, whom she had never met, who said so.

But Pam didn't want to ruin her last full day in the area, so she dismissed any thoughts of Jack, instead of focusing on what Gatlinburg had to offer her. As it turned out, she perused a part of town she hadn't seen and enjoyed an early dinner. It was not yet dark when Pam once again left the small town of Gatlinburg behind and drove away, being swallowed up by the mountain, where she rose almost to the top.

36

The sun had gone into hiding behind the mountains as Pam pulled up in front of her chalet. She had driven up the mountain with her lights on bright and had encountered nothing out of the way. Not even a deer. She looked around and saw nothing out of the way, so she removed the key from the ignition, unbuckled her seat belt, and opened the car door. The approaching darkness brought on a little nervousness, but she expected to feel better once she was safe inside the chalet. She hurried to the door, punched in the security code, turned the doorknob, and pushed open the door with her foot. She walked in. She was in the habit of leaving a light on each time she left, but evidently, she had forgotten to do that. Just as she reached for the light switch she saw a moving shadow. Her last thought before everything went black was that she should have gone in with her gun in her hand, not in her purse.

Pam woke up, felt a little funny. A little at a time she became cognizant of where she was, and what was going on. At first, her mind was only on her situation. She found herself seated in a chair, restrained. There was duct tape around her body, just below her chest, securing her to the chair in which she sat. As she began to take notice of her surroundings she could tell there was a dim light on, but the house wasn't flooded with light. As she was returning to normal, something caught her eye, slightly to her left and ahead of her. When it did, she jumped as much as her

203

restraints would let her. She noticed three figures seated on the couch. There was Jack, Bernie, and the man who had told her he was a police officer. She gasped as she noticed Jack had a knife in his chest, and the other two had been shot, one in the head, the other in the chest. Pam could tell that none of them had been shot while she was unconscious. The blood had dried and was too dark to be a recent wound. With each of the three people who ranked the highest on her suspect list suddenly eliminated, she wondered who could be responsible for the others' deaths and her being a prisoner. Had her attacker purposely not blindfolded her because he or she wanted Pam to know who wasn't responsible, and make her reevaluate her situation as she dreamed up new suspects?

Pam sensed the presence of someone behind her, but couldn't turn to see who it was. She wasn't sure turning was a good thing anyway because whoever was behind had probably killed the three men on the couch. Once her captor was certain Pam had seen the scene on the couch, whoever it was pulled Pam's head back, and started wrapping it with duct tape, beginning with the eyes. Pam was helpless. Her bound hands and legs kept her from fighting whoever was behind her. While Pam's captor covered her eyes over and over with duct tape, he or she didn't cover her nose or mouth, which allowed her to breathe normally.

Why did someone let her see the three men on the couch, and then cover her eyes? Pam could only think of two reasons why someone would have done that. The first was to frighten her even more than she was. Well, mission accomplished, but she would have been frightened anyway, knowing that her captor was with her. The other reason Pam was blindfolded was so that she wouldn't be able to identify her captor. Was it someone she knew or a total stranger Pam could describe to a police sketch artist? But if it was a stranger who didn't want to be seen, that would mean that whoever it was planned to release Pam. But why would someone murder these three men but let her live? The only reason Pam could think of is that the person had something against those three people, but didn't plan to harm anyone else. But if that was true, why come to the chalet at all? Why involve Pam in the charade? So it must be someone Pam knew. But who could it be? Her husband, his business partner, and the fake cop were dead. The only other people she knew in Gatlinburg, not counting anyone who had served her food in one of the area's restaurants, were the FBI agent and Carla. Was it one of them? As far as she knew, they didn't know each other. So she didn't think they were working together. She didn't see any way the two of them had formed a partnership. Besides, if the FBI agent wasn't a good guy, did that mean that everyone was bad? Pam could have believed that Carla might have been involved with Jack or Bernie, but not with someone she didn't know. And she didn't think Carla could have pulled this off by herself. Carla didn't even live in Tennessee, for whatever that was worth. But then she doubted that the man calling himself Hartsong lived in Tennessee, either. At least not in Gatlinburg. He claimed to be on vacation. Either he was on vacation, he was working on what he said he was working on, or he was up to no good.

Once Pam's captor was satisfied that she couldn't see and couldn't move, Pam heard the person move away and whisper to someone else in the room. That meant there were at least two bad people. Pam had trouble identifying one person it could be, let alone two. More than likely it wasn't anyone Pam knew.

Pam stopped thinking and listened as two pairs of footsteps moved around the room. If they were communicating, they were doing so by hand signals. True, they could have been texting, but she hadn't heard any fingers or thumbs on a cell phone. She thought that would make enough noise that she, only a few feet away and listening intently, would have heard it.

205

Pam listened. She heard a noise. It sounded like someone had walked over to the door leading to the deck and opened it. Why would they do that? She stopped wondering about the open door when she heard another noise. It sounded like the two of them were moving the coffee table. She knew people who rearranged their living room periodically, but this wasn't the time for something like that. She heard another noise like someone would make if they were lifting something. Yes, she was sure of it, and whatever it was, it was heavy enough that both people were needed to lift whatever it was.

Pam tried to remain still and not call attention to herself. Maybe if she could keep their minds on whatever it was they were doing, the cavalry would come and rescue her. What cavalry? The only possibility was the handsome stranger, who now claimed to be an FBI special agent. What if he was already in the room? Even if he wasn't, he always arrived in the morning. Even though she had been knocked out and couldn't see, she was fairly certain it was still nighttime. Of course, it was. She hadn't been knocked out after she saw the three dead men, and it was dark then.

Pam listened as the two people moved past her, a few feet apart as if each of them was carrying one end of the coffee table. And why move the coffee table? It wasn't as if they were making room for sleeping bags.

The captive woman continued to listen. The two people had walked past Pam. She assumed she didn't fit into their immediate plans. Well, at least not for a few seconds. She cocked her head, the way a bird does as if that would improve her hearing. The two people were moving away from her.

She heard another sound as if whatever it was they were moving they were carrying up the stairs. And then, someone made a misstep, maybe stubbed a toe and almost dropped the table. And someone a little too loudly said, "I'm sorry." The other person shushed the first one. Pam couldn't tell about the person who shushed the other one, but the "I'm sorry," sounded as if it was a woman's voice. A familiar woman's voice. But Pam couldn't tell who. It wasn't someone she saw every day, but then Pam didn't see any woman every day. She didn't work outside the home and didn't entertain much there. The maid did most of the work around the house. Pam did see her three times a week, but the voice she heard wasn't her maid. Still, it was familiar. She racked her brain trying to figure out who it was. Sometimes a voice or a face in unusual circumstances is harder to recognize. At least it was for Pam, but she had heard the person utter only two words, and that sotto voce, and several feet away from her.

After the one misstep, the project seemed to be going better, and whatever it was they were carrying up the stairs. Was it an object full of money? Were they carrying whatever it was upstairs because it allowed them to talk without Pam hearing them? At least as far as she could tell, she was the only other person alive in the house, other than her two captors.

Pam felt a breeze, remembered that one of her captors had opened the door to the deck. Here was her opportunity to shout for help. She evaluated her situation and felt certain that the movers would come to silence her long before the cavalry would come to her rescue.

The open door reminded Pam that she had planned to come back and spend some time in the hot tub. This made her mad. Quickly she forgot about her treat that wouldn't happen and listened to see if she could tell what was going on upstairs. As far as she could tell, both of her captors had made it all the way upstairs without suffering a heart attack. Maybe that meant that both of them were in fairly good shape. She was pretty sure that she could carry half of something of a reasonable weight.

She stopped thinking about how good of shape she was in when she heard another noise. This one came from through the open door to the deck and sounded like who-ever was upstairs had opened a door. Noises traveled well in the mountains on a fairly silent night. She heard a noise that sounded like a groan from upstairs, maybe a couple of groans followed closely by another sound. From what Pam, heard, it sounded like a crash, as if they had thrown some-thing into the trees and down the mountain. Pam shud-dered. There was no reason for someone to throw a table from the top level of a chalet, even if the table didn't go with the other furniture, but they might throw a body if they were evil enough and they didn't want anyone to find that body for a while. Was that to be Pam's fate? Was someone going to throw her over the upstairs railing?

Pam tried to free herself but to no avail. Even if she could loosen her restraints the two people upstairs would return before she could get away. With that hope snuffed out, she wished she could move over to the couch to see how many dead people were left, but then it was hard for her to get excited about feeling dead people to see if all three of them were left.

Again she struggled with her restraints, but couldn't even loosen them slightly. The duct tape held. Maybe if her captors left and left Pam where she was, she could move back and forth in the chair and loosen the duct tape, and eventually get free.

Pam had little time to reflect, because she soon heard the sound of footsteps coming down the stairs, a little more quickly than they had gone up the stairs. Pam froze as if doing so would make them forget that she was there.

Either they had made their plans upstairs or they were using hand signals to let the right hand know what the left hand was doing. One of them walked by her with a sure step, walked out on the deck, and walked toward the hot tub. The noise that followed was one that Pam had come to know. Someone was removing the cover of the hot tub. She wanted to be in the hot tub, but not this way. She wanted to go in on her own, and get out when she pleased. She tensed, wondering if the end was at hand.

Pam assumed there were more hand signals because whoever went out on the deck didn't stay there long enough to enjoy the view. That person returned, and if Pam was right that whatever they carried upstairs was a body, then body number two had just been picked up. If so, there was only one more body left before they got to her. Would they kill her first, or would they throw her in the hot tub with her hands and feet tied and put the cover back on it as they waited for her to drown. She didn't want to die. She felt like she had only begun to live in the last few days after she was free of Jack. Free of Jack. Was she free of Jack, and did she want to be free of him? She had suggested the vacation hoping to rekindle the feelings she felt were once there. But were there ever any feelings? And then she remembered that she was free of Jack. Dead men with knives in their chest don't come back to life without a little help from Jesus. And she didn't remember ever reading about a dead knife victim coming back to life, either in the Bible or the newspaper. Yes, she was free of Jack, whether she wanted to be or not.

The next sound Pam heard was someone baptizing the dead. Suddenly Pam had no interest in using that hot tub again. One body left. The cavalry still hadn't arrived. But then no one had summoned them. As far as Pam knew there were only three bodies. One had gone zip-lining without a zip line. One had just been immersed. And the other was sitting on the couch unable to enjoy the festivities. Pam's mind started getting weird. She wondered which one was Jack. Would Jack have been the one to be used as an object in the distance throw? Would he have liked to have gone clean? Or would he prefer to be the last to go? Pam knew she wanted to be the last to go, about forty years after the first three. Pam wondered if Jack was the one in the hot tub, and if so, would they put her in there

209

with him, sort of an until death do they part, and then some. Were they coming for her next? She prepared to scream as if that would do her any good.

Again Pam thought about who these two people were. She quickly added a name to her suspect list. Could it be the man who had called Jack the day before they left for the mountains? If so, did that mean that Jack was one of the two embezzlers and the man that called was either the person they had stolen the money from or someone who planned to blackmail Jack, and maybe Bernie, too?

Pam didn't have time to add any more names to her suspect list, because the duo came back in and sat down over in the breakfast area. Carrying two bodies is a tiring ordeal. Pam didn't know. She had never carried one body. The murderers didn't sit long, however, and soon it was evident that one of them remembered Pam was still there. The next thing Pam smelled made her cringe. At least it wasn't the smell of something burning. But she recognized the smell, and she knew that they wanted her to be unconscious when her time came.

Someone put a cloth loaded with ether over Pam's mouth and nose, and she could no longer hear their footsteps.

37

Pam stirred, but she was still enough out of it that she had no idea where she was or what had happened. That took a few more minutes to register. After those few minutes, she remembered the ordeal that she had endured. She couldn't believe she was still alive. But where was she? She hesitated, refrained from opening her eyes. But then she did and was surprised at what she saw. Had she been dreaming? It was dark outside, just like it was when she had experienced her nightmare. And she found herself seated in the same chair as she had sat in during her nightmare. Only there were no bindings. Nothing was keeping her from getting up out of the chair. But she didn't move. She looked around and it appeared that she was alone. The couch where she had envisioned the three dead people, one of whom was her husband, was empty. Was she so tired from her day that she had fallen asleep and imagined quite an ordeal in her mind?

She got up, walked over, and checked for bloodstains on the couch. There were none. Nothing in the room appeared to be out of place. She hurried upstairs. Nothing looked out of place there, either. The door to the deck was shut and locked, just like the one on the main floor. There was only one thing left to do and it terrified her. Still, she hurried down the stairs, unlocked the door leading to the deck, and hurried over to the hot tub. She remembered in her nightmare that her captors had put someone in the hot tub. It was time to check, to see if all of this was a figment of her imagination. She lifted the lid covering the hot tub and began to scream. The man who had come to her chalet posing as a policeman was floating in the water.

Pam dropped the lid back in place, not taking the time to see that it was on straight. She hurried back inside, rushed around, looking for the gun. She found it in her bag. After her captors had knocked her out and bound her they had failed to check to see if she was carrying a weapon. In a way that made sense. If whoever had left her in that dilapidated cabin were the same two people who had surprised her at the chalet, they wouldn't expect her to have a gun. They knew that they had taken her gun, and before they returned it they made sure that she couldn't use it again. And even if her attackers at the chalet were a different duo, they wouldn't expect her to have a gun. Most women on vacation don't carry guns. And no one who wasn't following her would think that she could have come up with another gun in Gatlinburg.

She checked the gun to make sure it was loaded. It was. It hadn't been fired. She didn't know if they would return for her, and if so, when. She felt safer with the gun, but she wasn't going to take time to pack. Maybe she would return with the police to get her things. But should she check to see if the third body was still on the premises? She decided not to do that.

She rushed to the door, stepped back and opened it with the gun pointed toward anyone who might rush inside. But no one did. There was no vehicle outside the chalet except her own. But then there was no other vehicle when she arrived. Somehow Pam didn't think that two people arrived on foot carrying three bodies. Whoever these people were, they stopped, unloaded the bodies, and one of them left to park around the next bend. But Pam had too much on her mind to wonder where her captors had parked. One of those things on her mind was where had they gone?

Maybe the twosome who had tormented Pam were long gone. Possibly well on their way to getting out of Tennessee. But Pam didn't want to assume anything, so cautiously she stepped out into the night, looked in every direction. When she saw no one she shut the door and took off running to her vehicle. She clicked the button and the doors unlocked. She walked around the SUV, looking in each seat, making sure there was no one inside. Once she was sure that she was alone, she opened the door, sat down, locked the vehicle, and put the key in the ignition.

She breathed a sigh of relief, then started the vehicle. The headlights came on automatically, and Pam hit the gas and took off. She tried her phone. No signal. Either she was too high up in the mountains or her phone needed charging. She wasn't sure where she was going, but she would use her GPS to locate the nearest police station, which she thought was at the bottom of the mountain, a few miles away, not far outside of Gatlinburg.

Pam put her lights on bright, just in case someone darted in front of her. A couple of minutes later she arrived at the first intersection, saw no lights from an approaching vehicle, and turned right without stopping. But it was late, and she didn't expect to encounter any traffic unless someone was lying in wait for her. But why would someone untie her, then lie in wait for her? It didn't make sense, so she focused on her nocturnal drive.

Pam had driven this road several times over the previous two weeks. She had learned somewhat about how the road lay and where the turns were. She knew the road would be relatively flat for a while, before it descended, just before arriving at the next road. She drove as fast as she could. allowing for the fact that there was a drop-off on both sides of the road. While people in Colorado might dispute her claim, as far as Pam was concerned she was on top of the world.

Pam drove on as fast as she could, braking each time she came to a curve, which was often. She encountered no other traffic, but the clock on the dash told her it was after 1:00. Her radio was on to help her keep her sanity. She was listening to music that was popular before she was born. 60s on 6. Sirius XM Radio. If there was any other sound, the music was loud enough to keep her from hearing it.

But the first thing that terrified her was not a noise. It was someone who had suddenly switched on their headlights, someone not far behind. The height of the headlights told her that it was possibly someone in a truck. Possibly two someones. With one indisposed body in the bed. A body in the bed of a truck doesn't cause as much attention after dark.

She didn't have time to think about who or what was tailgating her because the truck bumped her once, and then again a few seconds later. All of a sudden it was obvious to Pam who was following her and what they intended to do. Her captors had let her live, only because they wanted her to be overconfident and run her off the mountain. That way the police might think that she fell asleep while driving. The police would be more suspicious if they found her in the chalet with a bullet hole in her head. The same would be true if they found her in the hot tub with a dead man.

But who was it, and what had she done to them? Pam continued to drive, both hands on the wheel, going as fast as she could and remain on the road.

The truck behind her sped up, rammed her again, and remained there, bumper to bumper. Pam put her foot down hard on the brake and gripped the steering wheel with one hand, while she reached down and grabbed her gun with the other. She lifted the gun and fired over her shoulder, through the back window of the SUV, and possibly into the other vehicle. But whoever was driving the truck had floored his vehicle, which was causing her to go faster than she did before. She got off one other shot before her vehicle veered off the road and headed down the mountain. The drop where she went off wasn't as severe as some of the other drop-offs from the mountain. But she was headed down and her car was bouncing around on the uneven ground. Her foot had been on the brake ever since the truck had rammed her and remained on her bumper. The brake had done Pam no good before, and things hadn't improved. She fumbled for the emergency brake, but couldn't remember where it was. Instead of feeling for the dome light, she kept both hands on the wheel, trying to figure out which was the best direction to maneuver and stay alive. She wasn't sure which was better for her. To miss a tree and possibly plummet through the air, or to hit a tree, which might come through the windshield into her, or send her through the windshield toward it. She merely knew that at this point reverse was not an option.

She had no idea how far down the mountain she had traveled, but she looked up, saw a tree directly in front of her. The trees on each side kept her from going left or right. She rammed her foot into the floorboard once again and grabbed the seat behind her with both hands. At least the tree she was about to meet was small. But at impact, the tree sheared through the metal protecting Pam from it, and she didn't even want to think about what a larger tree would have done. She wondered if she would have been better off back in the hot tub with a dead man.

Upon impact, the airbag imploded. The vehicle stopped. And Pam was knocked a little silly, and for the third time that night and fourth time while on vacation she was unconscious.

38

Pam awoke. A minute or so later she realized where she was. It was still dark. She tried the dome light. It didn't work. She could see well enough to know that there was a tree almost between her legs, and that tree shouldn't have been there. The windshield was in little pieces, but for the time being, all of those little pieces were somehow still intact, forming a jigsaw puzzle in front of her.

She moved her head so she could look in the rearview mirror. Her neck hurt when she did, but she was able to see and see that the other vehicle wasn't headed her way on the hill behind her. She looked in the driver's side mirror but saw no one. She was headed down a mountain. Alone. And no longer moving.

She reached down to unbuckle her seatbelt. At least she was able to do that. She tried to lift her foot, but it was wedged in where the vehicle had been reconfigured, prohibiting her from moving it. She took stock of herself. As far as she could tell she had no broken bones, not even her foot, which wasn't even in pain. Oh, she felt pain. The airbag had left her chest feeling like it wasn't her best day, and her head had felt better. But from what she could tell, she wasn't bleeding. She was wedged into the driver's seat of her vehicle and didn't seem to be sitting on the edge of a precipice, which meant things could have been worse.

Maybe she was better off than being in a hot tub with a dead man.

She evaluated her situation. As far as she could tell she would live through the experience, provided that whoever caused her to go over the side of the mountain didn't come down to finish the job. Maybe they had slammed into another tree, or they could have navigated the mountain road, regained control of their vehicle, and were well on their way out of the area, figuring that she was dead. Well, she wasn't dead, but she was stuck. All she could do was hope that she had made enough of a mess when she left the road that one of the good guys would come looking for her. Whoever the good guys were. All she knew was that it was the middle of the night. She was stuck where she was. And she couldn't get away. She wondered if her captors had gotten away. She was too engrossed in her situation to know what direction the other headlights had headed. But she knew they hadn't headed down the mountain behind her. She guessed that meant that whoever was driving the other vehicle had been able to control his vehicle better than she had been able to control hers.

Unable to do anything else, she sat there, contemplating her situation. There was a slight chill coming in through the closed window, but nothing major. She didn't have anything to eat or drink, but so far she wasn't starved or thirsty. Still, it would have been nice to have had those three uneaten éclairs Hartsong had brought her, and a bottle of water.

Provided that Hartsong, or whoever the stranger was, wasn't the one who had rammed into her vehicle, she figured he would head to the chalet the next morning, and maybe he would search for her when he didn't find her there. Or would he assume that she had gone to Gatlinburg, and give her another day. But then that morning was when she was supposed to be checking out. Would he remember that?

Pam couldn't do anything about her predicament. She doubted that anyone would come for her during the night. She wondered if time would pass more quickly if she went to sleep. She wasn't sure but tested that theory and somehow was able to go to sleep.

+++

Pam awakened again. It was still dark, but she felt daylight wasn't more than an hour or so away. She remembered what had happened. The only thing she didn't know was who was responsible, and if they got away. She had no idea who it was. If she hadn't seen those three bodies back in the chalet she would have figured one or more of them was responsible. The only other person she could think of was Carla, and while she wondered from time to time whether Carla would try to steal someone's husband, she never figured her to be a murderer. But maybe Carla's voice was the female voice she had heard. But if so, who was the man, provided the other one was a man? Pam was upset and confused and not capable of improving her situation, so she went back to sleep.

+++

Sometime later, Pam was awakened when she heard someone shout and heard him tramping down the mountain toward her. If she heard correctly, it sounded like someone had said, "I've found her! Down here!" If so, that wasn't necessarily good news. It could be that her captors were insistent that she die. It might not do her any good to look. Even if she saw the man, she wouldn't know whether he was one of the good guys or not. But she would soon know. She tried to grab her gun but noticed it had fallen off down onto the floorboard. She was definitely at the mercy of someone who, from the sound of the footsteps, was coming down that mountain in a hurry whether he wanted to or not.

Whatever the case, it was daylight. Pam hadn't done anything to anyone else, so she hoped her ordeal would soon be over, and that the man rushing down toward her was one of the good guys. When he arrived a minute or so later, she didn't recognize him, and he didn't look intimidating. She felt that was a good sign. She turned the key in the ignition, tried to roll down the window, but that didn't work, either. She motioned to the man that the window wouldn't roll down. He would just have to shout through the glass.

"I'm with Smoky Mountain Fire & Rescue. Are you hurt bad?"

"I don't think so."

"Can you move?"

"My foot is wedged in the footwell, but I don't think it's hurt. I don't feel any pain."

"Touch your leg. Can you feel it?"

"Yes."

"And other pains?"

"Chest, head, and neck, but nothing seems to be major."

"Are you Mrs. Archer?"

"I am."

"I'm sorry we didn't get here sooner. Not long after daylight, someone reported you missing, and gave us an approximate location of where we might find you. There's not a major disturbance up top, but we saw some beaten-down grass and a grazed tree and decided to check it out. We wouldn't even have given it a second thought if we hadn't known someone was missing. Do you know what time you went over?"

"It was a little after 1:00."

"Well, it's a little after 8:00 now. You traveled quite a distance from where you left the road. A good two hundred feet or more. We're going to have to get a wench to get you out of here. We need to move your vehicle back a couple of feet so we can pry the door open and get you out. As it is, these trees on each side keep us from doing that and the rear of your vehicle is smashed in and I doubt if it will open. We'll try, but if not, we'll need to get that wench down here. I'll check out the back, and if it doesn't open I'll just step over there and call and let them know what we need. Then I'll be back to stay with you."

"I'm okay by myself if you need to do something else."

"No, I'm fine. But, as I said, we're about two hundred feet down. It'll take a few minutes to get you out. It's a good thing that the tree stopped you. Another ten feet and there's a severe drop-off, and if you went over you would have landed front first on the road down below. You might not think so right now, but you are one lucky lady."

Pam nodded and smiled, and the man walked away. A couple of minutes later the rescue worker stepped back over to her.

"They're on their way. It'll be a few minutes. We've got a stretcher, but the wench isn't here yet."

"A stretcher?"

"Yes, ma'am. Just to be on the safe side we're going to take you to the hospital. Get you checked out. You never know about internal injuries, and we always err on the side of caution. There's a good chance you won't be there more than a couple of hours."

"But I've got packing to do. I have to be out of that chalet today."

"Someone's working on that. After you get checked out at the hospital someone will come and see you there and get you up to date."

"Do you know who?"

"No, I'm just Fire and Rescue, but they'll take good care of you. I can assure you of that. Wait a minute. I'm getting a call."

The rescuer stepped away again, answered his call. He returned a couple of minutes later to inform her that the wench was on its way, and would be there in ten or fifteen minutes. After it arrived, it wouldn't be much longer until they would be able to free her.

39

A few minutes later the wench arrived and the line was let down to attach it to her car. It didn't take long to raise the vehicle up the hill a few feet, but a crowbar was needed to free Pam from her car. Then, as carefully as possible, two men lifted her from the car and strapped her to the stretcher, which they had to carry two hundred feet up the mountain. They were careful not to jostle her, and a second-team relieved them to finish the trek to the summit.

A little over thirty minutes after Pam was placed in the emergency vehicle she arrived at the hospital, was wheeled into a compartment in the emergency room, and someone came to check her vitals and take her information. They checked her for a concussion and internal injuries.

With no family to accompany her, she lay there wondering what had happened, and who was responsible. She had no idea. She couldn't blame the nurse who appeared periodically to check her vital signs or the doctor who came in to check on her. With a clear head and no interruptions, she still would have been unable to place the blame on any one person. There had to be someone that she didn't know about. As far as she knew, the two people who held her captive and then let her go so they could run her down had to have been someone she hadn't laid eyes on during her vacation. But she had no idea where to start. Could it have been the man who called her on the phone? Pam had no idea that before she left the hospital someone would be able to answer most of her questions.

It was three hours later, when all the tests had been completed and all the results studied, that the doctor came to inform Pam that she was sore but fine. They would be releasing her within an hour, but first, someone needed to talk with her. She assumed that someone was the police.

A couple of minutes after the doctor left Pam heard someone slide the curtain aside and step into the room. She looked up, saw who it was, and wasn't sure whether to smile or frown. Her visitor spoke first.

"I keep running into you in the most unique places."

"So, who are you today? A photographer, someone with a newspaper route, or a special agent with the FBI?"

"I'm afraid I'm still with the FBI. Disappointed?"

"I don't know. I've always had a thing for photographers."

"Well, I do have a camera. Would you like me to take some pictures, maybe put them on Facebook?"

Pam wrapped the sheet around her even tighter.

"I think I'll pass. Forgot to put on my makeup and all that."

"Well, we wouldn't want to inconvenience you, Mrs. Archer."

"So, you're turning over a new leaf."

"Something like that. Let's move on to why I'm here. What do you know about your situation?"

"Well, I know that my husband disappeared. I know that someone attacked me and held me captive in that ramshackle old cabin. I know that you showed up, just like you always seem to do."

"Why don't we move things along a little bit? Tell me about last night. What do you know about what happened, and who attacked you?"

"The who is what has me most puzzled. I'll start with when I got home. I pulled up. There was nothing that seemed out of sorts. No one outside. The first sign that things weren't the way they were supposed to be was when I opened the door and stepped inside. I always leave a light on, but this time the house was dark. I almost didn't have time to wonder if I had forgotten to do that or not, because almost immediately I was attacked. I should have been more careful and had my gun in my hand when I came in the door. Anyway, that didn't happen and seconds after I stepped into the house someone attacked and knocked me out. I think it was a blow to the head, but I'm not certain of that. What I do know is that sometime later I woke up and realized that I was confined to a chair. On the couch across from where I was sitting were three dead bodies seated on the couch. I recognized all three. There was my husband, his business partner, and the man who came to the chalet impersonating a police officer. My husband had been stabbed, still had the knife in his chest. The other two men had been shot. One in the head. One in the chest. I didn't have much time to think about that because almost immediately, someone came up behind me and started wrapping duct tape over my eyes. A few seconds later I couldn't see anything. Some of what happened after that is just speculation. But I believe there were two of them, a man and a woman. The woman whispered something to the man. Her voice seemed vaguely familiar, but I couldn't place it. I don't know if that was because of my situation, or there was another reason. I think whoever they were carried one of the bodies upstairs and threw it out over the balcony and down the mountain. I have no idea why they did this because a few minutes later they came back downstairs and picked up another body. But they didn't make the same concerted effort to get rid of this one. The second body they dumped in the hot tub. I know that is true because after I got free I went out and found the fake cop in the hot tub, dead. I have no idea what they did with the third body. I didn't see it again before I left and I didn't hear them when they disposed of it, because for some reason, they knocked me out again, this time with ether, and then I guess they left. When I woke up, I was no longer restrained. I picked up the gun I'd bought, which they had overlooked in my bag, and hurried out of the place. I had no idea at the time that all of this was a trap and they planned to kill me somewhere else. They had hidden someplace, probably at the end of my road with their lights off, and followed me when I left. Eventually, they caught up with me, because all of a sudden I saw bright headlights in the rearview mirror. I had the radio on and up high, so I didn't hear them coming. Anyway, after following me for a couple of minutes, they rammed me. I think they were in a truck, but I'm not sure of that. Anyway, after they had rammed me a few times and then stayed on my bumper. I was sure they were planning to kill me. I picked up the gun and fired a shot or two over my shoulder. I have no idea whether or not I hit anyone or anything because I lost control of my vehicle and plunged down the mountain. This happened a little after 1:00, and it was 8:00 before anyone found me. Is that what you wanted to know?"

"Pretty much, and I think that's great except for one or two things. However, it's an amazing recall for someone who has gone through what you went through."

"What two things? You mean I got a couple of things wrong or I left something out?"

"Mrs. Archer, from what you said, I assume you have no idea who held you captive or who was in that truck."

"That's what I said. None whatsoever. Everyone I thought of as a suspect was dead on that couch."

"Everyone but one."

"You mean you can read my mind and know who was on my list of suspects?"

"No, but I think I know who the dead people were on that couch."

"I know. I told you. I'm sure it was my husband, his business partner, and the guy who impersonated a cop. I had only a brief look at them, but I'm sure it was those three. So, did you catch them, or at least find the truck?"

"I'm afraid we did, Mrs. Archer. And I don't know how to tell you this, except to say that your husband was driving that truck. And Mrs. Carlucci was with him."

"But my husband is dead. He had a knife in his chest."

"Oh, I'm sure if you say he did, then he did. But did you know that Roz Carlucci used to do special effects for a low budget company in Hollywood? The knife was fake, and so was the blood. I'm sure her husband and the other man were dead. I've already been to the chalet. We had no idea until you told us just now where Bernie Carlucci is, or that he is dead, but we found the other guy in the hot tub. It helped that you didn't put the lid back on tight. And by the way, you didn't seem all that broken up when I told you that it was your husband."

"I guess I'm more relieved for all of this to be over than anything else. I'm not sure if Jack and I were ever in love. I thought this vacation might have been good for us, but then after that detective called. In the back of my mind, I suspected that Jack just brought me down here to kill me. So, did you catch him? Is he under arrest?"

"You might say we caught him, but he's not under arrest. You said that you shot back over your shoulder. Well, one of those shots hit him in the shoulder. Oh, it wasn't enough to kill him, but it did make him jerk the steering wheel and he ran off the road. He wasn't as fortunate as you. He ran into a tree, probably doing close to 50 m.p.h. Roz Carlucci was dead when we arrived. Your husband died on the way to the hospital. While we waited on the ambulance, I read him his rights, then accused him of murder and attempted murder. He denied both, said that you shot at him. But when I told him that we were doing a ballistic report on the bullet found in the dead man, and I bet him that it would match the bullets in his gun, he changed his tune. I think he suspected he was dying and had already seen his girlfriend die, so he confessed to everything. Well, maybe not everything. But enough. Although we didn't know about Bernie Carlucci being thrown from the balcony of your chalet until you told me. Up to that point, we had him listed as missing. We'll send a crew down for the body."

"So, what does this mean will happen to me?"

"Well, there I have some bad news for you. Your time in the chalet is over. We've already removed your things, and are holding them for you. Now, if you want, you can continue your vacation here, or you can go home."

"So, there are no charges against me?"

"Husbands and wives do some strange things sometimes. We don't know what your intentions were. For all we know, your husband asked you to tie him up and leave him there. Maybe he was preparing for survival camp or something. Anyway, whatever the case, we're willing to overlook the fact that you tied up your husband and left him in that cabin."

"I don't know what they were, either, although I doubt if I could have left Jack there for long. So, how did he get away, and who put me there?"

"As to how he got away, I'm pretty sure it was his girlfriend. The rest is speculation on our part. And from what we can ascertain, both partners were trying to kill the other. At least that's what your husband said, and from everything I can gather, that was the truth. Your husband said that someone tried to run over him not long before you two left to come down here. He thinks that Carlucci hired someone to do that. Your husband admitted that he and Mrs. Carlucci had been carrying on for well over a year. He didn't know if her husband knew or not, but he admitted that he and Bernie Carlucci hadn't gotten along and hadn't trusted each other for some time. Another thing. Almost everyone known to mankind had a tracer on the back bumper of your vehicle. I'm surprised that each new person who put one there didn't find the ones that were already there. But I guess that you made things easier for Bernie Carlucci, only his wife got there to rescue your husband before her husband got there to kill him, or sent someone else to do the job. She was actually in the area before you arrived. Anyway, from what I've learned about Carlucci, I think he would have murdered your husband if he had found him there. Our handwriting expert is pretty sure that Carlucci is the one who left the notes for you, hoping that you could lead him to your husband. We found one of his prints at the cabin, so we assume that he was the one who tied you up. He didn't care whether you lived or died, so he left you there and let the circumstances decide your fate. My guess is he got a little careless, and he and the man who impersonated a cop, who was working for Carlucci, got shot before he could shoot your husband."

"And what did you find out about Jack having a former life?"

"We think your husband and Carlucci were the embezzlers, but now that they're dead, we're not sure we want to pursue it any further. The company received restitution from the insurance company. The insurance company gave up on the matter a few years ago. So we're not sure that we need to spend valuable time checking on two men who won't serve time if we find out they were guilty."

"And what about Carla?"

"From everything we can tell, she was just a woman who wanted to do her job right. She was worried that something might have happened to your husband, but we've not been able to come up with any evidence that she was aligned with either man or had anything to do with anything that happened to you. I don't think your husband was carrying on with two other women, just Carlucci's wife."

"Any idea who the other stranger was in the Pancake Pantry? The one that looked like a dangerous criminal?"

Hartsong chuckled and removed a couple of photographs from a plastic bag in his pocket.

"Is this the man you're talking about?"

"So, you're familiar with him."

"Yeah, he's another agent. We work together sometimes. And just to make sure, is this the man you referred to as the cop impersonator?"

"That's him. Are you going to tell me he's another agent?"

"No, he's a small-time gun for hire. Or at least he was. We've suspected him of several jobs, but we've never been able to pin anything on him. Looks like we won't have to now."

"Speaking of now, what do I do now?"

"Well, my suggestion would be that you get dressed. I know from a couple of trips to your place that you don't always wear a lot of clothes, but if you try running around here in what you've got on now you might get arrested. Then, from the looks of that vehicle of yours, I think you might need to rent another one. I guess that yours is totaled. I can take you to a car rental place, or if you'd rather have the criminal-looking agent do that, I can arrange for that to happen, too. But what you do is up to you. The hospital should release you in a few minutes. I've got the place where I'm staying on River Road holding a room for you, in case you want it."

"I'll take it. There's no way I'm going back home today. I might even stay a few more days. Are you willing to deliver meals to an invalid?"

"Well, the room is yours as long as you want it. You're paying for it, of course. And are you sure you want meals delivered by someone you can't trust?"

"I think all the ones I can't trust are dead now. Oh, I'll probably check in and get some rest today, spend a little more time here tomorrow and maybe another day or two, say goodbye slowly, and then get home when I'm feeling a little better. So, where do you live? And is there a wife back home?"

"I live in Louisville, and I lied about the wife part, too. There's no way a woman would want to live with a man who takes pictures and has a paper route."

"Oh, I wouldn't be too sure about that. Now, being married to an FBI agent is another matter."

"Special agent."

"So, what does a special agent do?"

"Special things."

"Like rescue captive women from dilapidated cabins?"

"Among other things."

"Well, feel free to give me one of your cards, just in case I need a special agent someday."

"I think I can arrange that."

40

Special Agent Hartsong walked out, and a couple of minutes later a nurse came in to tell Pam that she was being released and could get dressed. Hartsong was still there when she walked out of the emergency room and she accepted his offer of a ride to the hotel where he was staying. Neither of them spoke much on the way to the hotel, as Hartsong could tell the woman was thinking about what her new life would be like. Hartsong dropped her off and helped her into the lobby. There he handed her the room key and she shook his hand and thanked him for what he had done, and apologized for not trusting him from the beginning. He reminded her he would be back at mealtime so that she would be dressed for a change.

+++

Pam didn't know what to think. Not only didn't her husband love her and had been carrying on with another man's wife for over a year, but he had tried to kill her. She decided to think of it as a cancer that had been removed, and hoped that she could forget all about Jack Archer, just as soon as she made one phone call.

She checked into her room with a view overlooking Little Pigeon River and stepped out onto the balcony to enjoy the view, and make her phone call.

"Hello. Are you still alive?"

231

"I just called to let you know that you were right."

"Who is this? You sound like my daughter. But she would never admit that I'm right."

"I think it's the first time, but you were right."

"You mean the detective was right? That scumbag Jack was trying to kill you?"

"Afraid so."

"So, have they arrested him?"

"No, but somebody will have to make burial arrangements."

"You mean you killed him first?"

"Nope. He ran into a tree trying to run me off a mountain."

"Now, I know you're kidding."

"Honest, Mom. And he killed his partner Bernie and another guy, too. And he had this thing going on with Bernie's wife. Oh, Bernie and the other guy were trying to kill him, too."

"Boy, nice company you're keeping."

"You mean the FBI guy?"

"So, was he with the FBI?"

"Yeah, and not married."

"So, are you going after him, or let him catch you?"

"I don't know. In the morning I'm going back to that breakfast place where I saw him a few times before. I'm sure he'll show up if he's interested. Just in case, I'll let him know that's where I'm going and what time I'll be there."

"Okay, but remember, that smart detective is mine."

"Sounds fine, Mom. You saw him first. See you in a couple of days."

+++

Pam ended her call, spent a couple more minutes looking down upon the Little Pigeon River, than shut the sliding glass door, closed the drapes, and lay down to take a nap. She'd had quite an ordeal. She wasn't going out that day. Nick Hartson would be bringing food to her. Then she planned to go to bed early, and then enjoy another day or two in the mountains if she felt up to it before going home and beginning her new life.

+++

Pam walked into Pancake Pantry and looked around. There wasn't an FBI agent anywhere. At least not one she recognized. She sighed and was seated. She wasn't sure if she wanted him to be there or not. At least she wasn't sure until she looked up and saw him leaning over the banister, looking down at her. Her face flushed. And then she smiled, but he was gone. Had he been there, or did she imagine it? She looked around but didn't see him anywhere, so she studied the menu to see what she wanted for her last breakfast in Gatlinburg.

"I understand the crepes are good here. Is this seat taken?"

It was everything she could do to keep from standing up and embracing him.

"I was saving it for a handsome stranger."

"How about if I take it until he arrives. I'm bushed. I had a hard time delivering all my newspapers this morning."

"I don't think you have any problem with your delivery."

He smiled at her remark.

"You know, I'm going to miss you."

"You don't have to. Lexington isn't that far away. Just over an hour from Louisville."

"And it probably would seem shorter if you were excited about why you are going there."

"And longer if you are the one waiting."

233

Pam thought about asking for a pitcher of ice water so she could pour it over her head and cool off. She thought anyone nearby would think the two of them were acting like high school kids.

+++

The two of them enjoyed a delicious breakfast, and Nick Hartsong remained with her while she went shopping in The Village shops and made some purchases, including a Thomas Kincaid print she had fawned over on her first trip there, which they promised to ship to her. She made a few other purchases including donuts and candy. When she finished, Nick informed her that he still had more work to do on the case before heading home the next day. He carried her things back for her. She was feeling better after a good night's sleep, so she thanked him, gave him her phone number, and headed upstairs to pack and check out.

+++

As Pam was packing, her phone rang. She checked to see who it was, but the ID said "Unknown Caller." Curious, she answered.

"Mrs. Archer."

"Who is this?"

"I talked to you a couple of weeks ago on behalf of the Berium Corporation. Remember, I was trying to reach your husband."

"How did you get this number?"

"It's a listed number."

"No, it's not. But I can now tell you that I know that the Berium Corporation is no more. And both of the two men whose names you gave me are dead. So are my husband and his partner. I am now the sole owner of Archer &

234

Carlucci, and I'm not interested in talking to you about any thing."

"But Mrs. Archer, your husband and I had a deal."

"No, you didn't. Listen, I know about the large sum of money that was embezzled several years ago. I also know that the insurance company has paid the company and that neither of them is pursuing this matter anymore. I suspect that you think my husband was responsible, and that you were trying to blackmail him. Well, as I said, my husband is no longer alive. You can verify that if you want. Bernie Carlucci is also dead. So is his wife. And I'm not interested in talking to you. But if you wish to talk to someone else about this I suggest you call Special Agent Nick Hartsong of the FBI in Louisville. He knows all about the case. Should you call me back instead, I will contact Special Agent Hartsong and have him find out who you are and get in touch with you. Are we clear on this? Now, goodbye."

For the first time in years, Pam felt good about herself. She also felt secure in her position. She smiled as she thought of how she treated the man who was trying to blackmail her husband and she was sure that he wouldn't be calling her again.

+++

Pam finished packing and checked out of the hotel. She loaded everything in the car she had rented. She had three places she wanted to visit before she left the Smoky Mountain area behind. Her last stop would be in Sevierville, on the north side of Pigeon Forge. She had promised someone that she would eat at the Applewood Farmhouse before she left town. When she got there, after making her other two stops, she was glad someone had told her how to find it, because even though it was only a short distance off the main road in a place that looked like out in the country, it couldn't be seen from the main road by the thousands of people who traveled that road each day.

But that was to be her last stop. Her first stop was one of Pigeon Forge's newest attractions, a Ferris wheel twenty stories high where people sat enclosed in gondolas while they rode and saw what the area looked like from well up above. The experience made her feel like a kid again.

Her second stop was someplace she had been before on her trip, but this time she was on a buying spree. She parked in the lot outside The Incredible Christmas Store and went inside. Before she left, she purchased three Christmas trees, and lots of ornaments for each one, which she instructed them to ship to her home. While Christmas was still several months away she felt the odds that she would celebrate Christmas were very good. And as she drove away and looked at all reminders of the Smoky Mountains in her rear-view mirror, she vowed to return to the area. Why not? Everyone who wished her dead was already dead. Maybe next time she could come with another husband, maybe an ex-FBI special agent. After all, soon she would be coming into a lot of money. She preferred a happy marriage to money, but who says that she couldn't have both. Only time would tell, and it looked like she would have more of that than seemed likely a couple of days earlier.

Author's Note: Are you ready for another mystery full of suspense, but with different characters? Check out *Murder in the Dark*.